STE
Nαι

AMERICA BLOWING IN THE WIND

GOD BLESS
WITH YOUR
CHRISTIAN FAITH

AMERICA BLOWING IN THE WIND

DON W. ROBERTSON

TATE PUBLISHING
AND ENTERPRISES, LLC

America, Blowing in the Wind
Copyright © 2016 by Don W. Robertson. All rights reserved.

No part of this publication may be reproduced, stored in a retrieval system or transmitted in any way by any means, electronic, mechanical, photocopy, recording or otherwise without the prior permission of the author except as provided by USA copyright law.

This book is designed to provide accurate and authoritative information with regard to the subject matter covered. This information is given with the understanding that neither the author nor Tate Publishing, LLC is engaged in rendering legal, professional advice. Since the details of your situation are fact dependent, you should additionally seek the services of a competent professional.

The opinions expressed by the author are not necessarily those of Tate Publishing, LLC.

Published by Tate Publishing & Enterprises, LLC
127 E. Trade Center Terrace | Mustang, Oklahoma 73064 USA
1.888.361.9473 | www.tatepublishing.com

Tate Publishing is committed to excellence in the publishing industry. The company reflects the philosophy established by the founders, based on Psalm 68:11,
"The Lord gave the word and great was the company of those who published it."

Book design copyright © 2016 by Tate Publishing, LLC. All rights reserved.
Cover design by Albert Ceasar Compay
Interior design by Shieldon Alcasid

Published in the United States of America

ISBN: 978-1-68293-230-8
1. Religion / General
2. Religion / Christian Life / Spiritual Warfare
16.08.15

My deceased first wife, Doris M. Robertson
(1940–1993)

My deceased second wife, Nancy M. Robertson
(1935–2011)

My deceased oldest son, Don W. Robertson
(1962–2009)

My son Brad S. Robertson and his wife,
Teresa Kuss Robertson

My daughter, Loretta E. Robertson

My dear friends Rev. Frank Bunn and his wife,
Mary Ellen Bunn

My dearest family and friends

My special friends of Pacesetters

The American military and veterans

And the people of Heritage Pointe, Senior Living Community, Cookeville, Tennessee—this is where I live.

Preface

GOD LAID IT on my heart to write my book, *America, Blowing in the Wind.* He gave me the ideas and the words. Praise the Lord. This book is broken into three parts. The first part is about what has happened to our great America in my lifetime of the past eighty-plus years. The second part covers the 1960s to the Rapture of His Church, and the third part is about what will happen after the Rapture of the Church. We are living in the end-times or last days of this church age. For I can feel it, hear it, and see it in the last several years. The lifetime of a country or a nation is about two hundred to three hundred years before it hits its financial and military peak. I believe that our great America has hit those peaks. God has bless our country for many years; now our country is changing, with decaying Christian morals, bad business and government ethics, and a broken-down federal government leadership that has pushed it to bankcruptcy. Only God can bless and heal our America again, only if His people will believe in God and pray.

> If my people, who are called by my name, will humble themselves and pray and seek my face and turn from their wicked ways, then will I hear from heaven and will forgive their sin and will heal their land.
>
> —2 Chronicles 7:14

1

THE HISTORY OF our country over the last four hundred years was based upon Christian beliefs, with people as the following: the Pilgrims coming to the New World, the early settlers forming the thirteen colonies, the Founding Fathers of 1776, the pioneers going across the plains into the Rocky Mountains onward to the West Coast, farmers and ranchers of the Heartland sowing seeds for the breadbasket to feed the hungry and starving people of the world, the hardworking men and women in all different jobs, our brave military and veterans, and the honest leadership of business and government. These people were the real backbone in providing the heartbeat of America.

Freedom of religion was the main purpose of the people coming to America. It was because of their faith that we have freedom of the press, freedom of religion, and freedom of speech. These three freedoms are the main reasons that our God has blessed our country for so many years. God has always blessed His faithful children and their family, for God wants His children to keep on believing for our America.

Since the 1960s, I have been seeing bigger changes in our country: the decaying ethics and morals from leaders in our business world, the leaders in our federal government, and the citizens of this great nation. Yes, we are living in the end-times or the last days of this church age.

These are the words that our Founding Fathers believed:

> I believe in the United States of America as a government of the people, by the people, for the people, whose just powers are derived from the consent of the governed; a democracy in a Republic; a sovereign Nation of many sovereign states; a perfect Union, one and inseparable; established upon those principles of freedom, equality, justice, and humanity for each American patriots sacrificed their lives and fortunes.
>
> I therefore believe it is my duty to my country to love it, to support its Constitution, to obey its laws, to respect its flag, and to defend it against all enemies.

On this journey, we will be seeing many pumps on the way, danger curves ahead, or going in the wrong direction. Yes, there are smooth highways for us to travel or at times like traveling in those crazy fast lanes. Just take time to stop at various rest parks on this journey, its call "Stop and smell the Roses." So many people are travel in the fast lane, going no where. These are just a few of the likeable ups and downs on our journey of where our America has been or maybe going.

In my eighty-plus years, I have seen lots of changes in my lifetime. I was born during the Great Depression years, in a farmhouse that was owned by my mother's grandparents, which was located near a small farming community in New Maysville, Putnam County, Indiana. Those were real hard times during the 1930s that our country was facing, my dad making one dollar per day in farm wages by working from sunup to sundown. Thank goodness we had free housing, and my mother canned from the garden; plus we had chickens and a time for hog killing. Those were the days when everybody we knew had very little. We were blessed with having what we had; that was the way it was during those hard-time years.

When World War II broke out, we moved to a county seat town, Danville, Hendricks County, Indiana. I lived in Danville with my parents and my sister for the next twelve years. After graduating from Danville High School in 1953, I enlisted in the US Army by going to their Finance School. Served my country for the next three years. I was stationed at Fort Leonard Wood, Missouri (basic training);

Fort Harrison, Indiana (Finance School); Fort Carson, Colorado (First Finance Office); and the Eighth Army Headquarters, Seoul, Korea (Twenty-First Finance Office). Real proud of being an American veteran by serving my country during those three years. Took my GI Bill; got a BS degree in accounting from Ball State University, Muncie, Indiana; graduated the class of 1960. I was married to my first wife for thirty-two years, and we had two sons and one daughter. I worked as an accountant for thirty-three years which was mostly at Dana Corporation, a large auto-truck supplier, retiring in 1993. I took an early retirement from work to take care of my first wife, who was dying of colon cancer. I was single for the six years, meet my second wife and we were married for twelve years until she died in 2011.

My two deceased wives, Doris M. Robertson and Nancy M. Robertson, and my oldest deceased son, Don W. Robertson, and the rest of our family were faithful strong Christians. I always believed in being faithful, having a good education, working hard, and being a good husband and parent—these are the kinds of qualities that make a better and stronger America. Our good God will keep blessing this country only with believing, faithful Christian people for they are the true cornerstones and the foundation for our America. This is the main reason that our country can and will go forward in financial greatness and be a military world power country.

My generation of people lived better than my parents, and they lived better than their parents, because we are living in a time of having a better standard of living and having a good education. My generation hit the peak years of the 1990s, having secure, good-paying jobs and related benefits consisting of health care insurance and retirement plans. The retirees of my generation are being blessed with both Medicare and Social Security programs to take care of us in our golden years. Now the present and the future generation of Americans of this new twenty-first century will be facing their future lacking a good job security and good medical care coverage, underfunded company and local-state-federal government pension plans, and soon a bankrupt Medicare, Medicaid, and Social Security System. The main reason for these uncertain conditions and times is that our America is financially bankrupt, with a broken-down federal government. Americans in the future will have to adjust to a different or lower standard of living. Also, we are living and working in a competitive world economy; that can change your standard of living anytime. Because of 9/11, America and rest the world must be on guard all the time for any terrorist alerts and attacks. It will not get any better, so always be on alert, prepared, and be ready for any changes that will be coming up during your lifetime.

I recall the days when the people of America feel safe anytime and anywhere in their community and homes, the following being some of the reasons: not having to lock their cars and homes anytime, children playing in their yards day or night in safety, picnics in the park, Sunday drives after church, feeling free to walk into town for a good movie at the Royal Theater, families gathered around the radio during the 1930s through the 1940s to hear their favorite programs. Then the 1950s was the black-and-white TV family programs and going to school for a good and safe education. There were no major crimes during the 1940s and 1950s in our hometown of Danville, Indiana. Those were the good old days; they will never return. The kind of world we have and see today, if it doesn't change in the near future for the better in God's eyes, we will be seeing our great America, blowing in the wind.

I recall the twelve years living in Danville, Indiana. It was a county seat town of Hendricks County, which was located about twenty miles west of Indianapolis. Back in the 1940s through the 1950s, there were no major crimes in our hometown or in the county. The Hendricks County sheriff and his two deputies had few problems keeping law and order. The county jail had no more than fifteen cells, with no inmates most of the time. The town of Danville had only two part-time town marshals for the day shift and one for the night shift. What a big difference between life of those yesteryears compared to that of today, with all kinds of major crimes on the increase, which are mostly alcohol or drug related. We see the county jails and the federal and state prisons are always full with inmates.

During the 1920s, everyone—from the local barber, to the shoeshine boy, to the taxicab driver—had a stock tip. Their stock hot tip might be to buy General Electric, General Motors, National Cash Register, RCA; Sears, Roebuck & Company; or US Steel; be sure to buy low and sell high. Those Roaring Twenties happy days all came to an end on October 29, 1929, when the stock market crashed, marking the beginning of the Great Depression years, with stocks of the Dow Jones Industrial Average declined almost 90% in value from a high of 381 on September 1929. By November 13, 1929, the loss in devalued stocks was about $13 billion. It was big-time greed by investors buying stocks at 10% margin with borrowed money.

The Great Depression was a worldwide economic crisis. As consumers lost buying power from being unemployed, construction and industrial production fell throughout the 1930s. It was a time in America when people were saying, "Say, mister, can you spare a cup of coffee?" or "Will work for a meal." Both the poor and rich people were sharing the same soup and unemployment lines. There were banks and business failures, savings accounts wiped out, foreclosures by the millions, unemployment of 25 percent, and the farmers and ranchers were facing tougher times. It was a time that most Americans were facing harder times and adjusting to a different and lower standard of living for the next ten years of the 1930s.

Farmers were caught in a depression of their own throughout most the 1930s. This was caused by the collapse of food prices with the lost export market after World War I. Then came the 1930s' drought years, which was marked by large dust storms that blackened the skies across the plains, plus the loss of rich topsoil that was blowing in the wind. In cities and towns, people lost their homes, and the farmers lost their land and equipment by means of bankruptcy or foreclosures.

President Franklin D. Roosevelt served four terms (1933–1945) for our America. He was the most influential president of the twentieth century. The new president established government programs for the purpose of controlling the depression. One such program was the New Deal, which would prevent further economic instability and promote the growth needed to end the Great Depression. Its main purpose was that of relief, recovery, and reform through the National Recovery Administration (NRA). The slogan of that time was "We Do Our Part." The idea was that the federal government would play an active role in the economy by joining forces with business and labor for a good working relationship.

The NRA set out to organize the national economy, industry by industry, to organize prices, wages, and promote competition. Such planning would prevent further economic instability and promote the growth needed to bring the Great Depression to an end as soon as possible.

FDR's fireside chats on radio provided confidence and reassurance to many Americans in both rural and urban regions of the country. More people supported the New Deal program, which was a good sign for the future of our country, and that the president was doing a good job. A good American president must stand firm with sound confidence for his country in any bad situation, such as that of hard financial conditions or in the time of war.

2

It was President Roosevelt's words heard by millions as Americans gathered around their radio regarding the attack on Pearl Harbor. Those were heartbreaking times as the country came out of the Great Depression years into the unknown conditions of World War II. Everyone turned up their RCA radios to hear what the president had to say:

> Yesterday, December 7, 1941, a date of which will live in infamy, the United States of America was suddenly and deliberately attacked. With confidence in our armed forces, with the absconding determination of our people, we will gain the inevitable triumph, so help us God.

World War II might be the only war that our America had ever fought across two different oceans, the Atlantic and the Pacific. Those two wars were so far away from our homeland. This war took place during a time of so many big unknown changes for our America, fighting two major wars—with Germany in Europe and with Japan in the Pacific Islands. Many brave, dedicated, and faithful men died in several battlefields or were wounded in action as they fought for our freedom and liberty for the future generations of Americans. The number of American fighting men that died from the war was an estimated 405,000 and an estimated 671,000 were wounded. The financial cost of World War II was estimated to be about $300 billion, or $4.3 trillion in today's dollars. These fighting heroes are known as the "Greatest Generation."

Numerous battles were fought during World War II. Some of the battles lasted only days, while others took months. Some of the major battles of this war are the following: Battle of the Atlantic, Budge, Iwo Jima, Midway, Normandy, Okinawa, Pear Harbor, and so many others.

Wars of the past or those of the future, freedom is not free, and it always comes with a price—both financial and with the loss of military troops and other people's lives. May our God in heaven bless those fighting heroes and the veterans of all wars.

World War II was another time for Americans to give up their wants and needs in life by working as a team to bring the two wars to an end as soon as possible. Men were drafted or enlisted for the armed services; they wanted to serve their country. It was a time for "Uncle Sam

Wants You" posters in this time of need. Hometown folks purchased consumer goods and gas with ration books/ stamps, buying US war bonds, planting victory gardens in their backyards, recycling of any kind of metal and rubber products for the war, reducing speed limit to 40 mph on highways, and women working in factories building war products such as ammunition, guns, planes, ships, and tanks. Those hardworking women on the factory assembly lines became known as Rosie the Riveter. Women served in various organizations such as the American Red Cross and the USO, and some women enlisted in the armed services. The factory workers had a slogan for that time: "Pass the ammunition and praise the Lord."

The farmers of America's Heartland were exempted from the armed services for the sole purpose of providing food for the servicemen and servicewomen, plus feeding the hometown folks across America. President Franklin D. Roosevelt and later President Harry S. Truman had to make hard decisions during those troubled times. Our country came out of back to back hard times of the Great Depression years of the 1930's into the two wars of the early to the mid 1940's years.

After the death of President Roosevelt in 1945, his vice president, Harry S. Truman, became the next American president. It was the new president's great leadership that brought World War II to a quicker end by using the atomic bomb against Japan. Those were hard decisions by President

Truman during those those troubled times, but there was no other way; and the final result was that it saved more military personnel and other people's lives and reduced the financial cost of war.

Over three years after the end of World War II, those brave fighting heroes that fought for world freedom and liberty were coming back home. This was the time for hometown parades coming down Main Street across America, with the bands playing Victory songs, crowds waving American flags, and big signs in store windows saying "Welcome Home" and "We are Proud." The end of the war brought thousands of servicemen back to America, as they pick up their lives and start new families, with the new job of building up America again.

The GI Bill was a big plus for the country. Men and women were going back for higher education and obtaining financial loans for their dream homes. It was a time for families being together again, time for talking about the good times, playing with children in the yards, going on picnics in the park, "Let's do something this summer," and going to Grandma's for the holidays. During those troubled times, our country came together as a working team for the main purpose of making America greater and stronger. This was a time in our country for saying those great words of "Praise the Lord and God Bless America," and "We are the land of the brave and the free," and of being proud to be an American.

During the 1940s, there was very little family leisure time. Mostly, the family gathered around their radios in the evenings and listened to their favorite programs. Those radio programs had outstanding sound effects, making you feel that you were part of the adventure program, or being at the musical or at the comedy show. The top radio and television programs at that time were the following:

For adventure, we had *Gang Busters*, *The Green Hornet*, *Inner Sanctum*, and *The Lone Ranger*; for sports, there were baseball games and the Friday night boxing fights from Madison Square Garden. The big-time comedy shows were *Amos 'n' Andy*, *The Bob Hope Show*, *Fibber McGee and Molly*, *Burns and Allen*, and *The Red Skelton Show* closing with "Good night and may God bless."

People loved country music from Nashville, Tennessee, which was played on radio station WSM of the Grand Ole Opry, with singing stars such as the Carter Family and Jimmie Rodgers. Yes, there were good times on weekends for round and square dancing: just clap your hands and kick up your heels to the country/western music. Bob Hope and so many others played a big part in the war by going overseas with their hit shows, providing lots of laughs and music by entertaining our American troops.

The other family pleasure was going to the movies; there in Danville, Indiana, on the east side of the square, was the Royal Theater. The Hollywood movies of the 1930s through the 1950s were not rated as the ones of this twenty-first century. I have listed some of the good ole movies from the yesteryears. These are the real Hollywood classics that are still being enjoyed years later as TV reruns. The 1930s movies were *Gone with the Wind*, *Snow White and the Seven Dwarfs*, *The Wizard of Oz*; and there were some great classic westerns like *Stagecoach*. So many classic musical shows from the 1930s into the early 1950s were outstanding with Gene Kelly in *Singin' in the Rain* or Fred Astaire dancing with Ginger Rogers in the movies *Roberta* and *Top Hat*.

The best 1950s movies were *The African Queen*, *Ben-Hur*, *The Bridge on the River Kwai*, *Friendly Persuasion*, *From Here to Eternity*, *Seven Brides for Seven Brothers*, and the western movies *High Noon* and *Shane*.

I saw many movies at the Royal Theater over those twelve years while living in Danville, Indiana. Each Sunday and Monday evening was one movie, different movie on Tuesday and Wednesday evening, the big double feature on Thursday, Friday, and Saturday evenings, which always included a western. I must have seen over six hundred of those cowboy western movies. Great movie enjoyment for a price of a quarter plus a candy bar or a sack of popcorn for a nickel. Those good ole days will never return.

Those classic movies of years ago were the best of the best, with great actors and actresses. How sad that in the last several years Hollywood movies have become rated PG, R, or X—this is what attracts the present-day moviegoers.

The good news is we still can see those classic movies as reruns on the Turner Classic Movies channel (TCM). The old-time movies of years ago are the vanishing America, just blowing in the wind.

During my grade school years, I was a very backward and shy kid. I came out of that shyness in my junior high years and got more interested in book learning by becoming a better student. I received a good high school education with teachers that had an interest in their students. Those were the days when teachers were involved with their profession so that students were learning more. It was a time when students had respect for their teachers and teachers had respect for their students. During my senior year of high school, I took a bookkeeping class under Mr. Guy Maham. It was through his teaching that I got turned on, and years later, I went into a career as an accountant. Some of my other high school teachers were Mrs. Armstrong, Mrs. Clay, Mrs. Gilham, Mr. Franklin, Mr. Kirley, and Coaches Robert Leedy (basketball/baseball) and Moe Moriarty (football/track). There were only forty-two students in our 1953 Danville high school class, which was the largest graduating class in Hendricks County that year. Our Danville High School classmates always had a close relationship, and we still do after sixty-two-plus years. We have our annual dinners/reunions of those who are able and want to come. This is true friendship—keeping in touch with your high school classmates over the years.

The last three years of my high school days saw the Korean War, which went on from June 25,1950, until July 27,1953. It started as a civil war between Communist North Korea and the Republic of South Korea. This was one of America's least popular war. So many American soldiers were killed, wounded, or became MIA or POWs. Because of this unpopular war, an estimated 37,000 American fighting heroes lost their lives, and an estimated 103,000 were wounded. The financial cost to America was at an estimate of $30 billion. Yes, we learned again the hard way that freedom is not cheap. My Americans across our great land, always be proud of our fighting heroes and the veterans of all wars.

After the war, servicemen came home to start families, moving into the suburbs and working at jobs manufacturing consumer goods for our America. They took their GI Bill and went back for their education, and financed their dream homes. For myself, I did the same thing when I came home from Korea in the fall 1956. Marched off to Ball State University in Muncie, Indiana, and obtained a BS degree in accounting, graduating with the class of 1960. Those American veterans were building a better country for the next generation. We must take the time to honor and remember our military and the veterans of all wars. My Americans, always believe in your country during both the bad and the good times. We must always have our chest out and our chin up, and stand tall by working together as a team for a greater America.

The people of the 1950s drove those big fancy V8 engine cars going to the drive-in movies and the drive-in restaurants. Each fall season, people went down to the local car dealers to see the latest in new car styling. Yes, the 1950s were the best of times for those great–looking, powerful cars. It was like a game of show and tell. It was a time when Chevy and Ford were competing for number one in car sales for each year. The auto companies Chrysler, Ford, and General Motors had almost 90 percent of the car/truck market. The final result: the smaller car companies such as Hudson, Kaiser-Frazer, Nash, Packard, and Studebaker were blowing in the wind. Those classic cars of the 1950s are still seen in many car shows or in car museums as collector's items, for they are one of a kind. During those years, the price of gas was about a quarter per gallon, plus free full services of cleaning the windshield, looking under the hood to check your battery and oil, and putting free air in the tires. Big *wow*—those were real services.

The 1950s was a big change for our America, with some of the following events:

- The Billy Graham Evangelistic Association was founded in 1950.
- The Dwight D. Eisenhower presidency (1953–1961).
- The Interstate Highway System was authorized in 1956.

- The African-American Civil Rights Movement of 1955–1968 opened the doors for all Americans to an equal and fair education regardless of creed, race, and religion.
- America launched *Explorer 1* into outer space 1957.
- Alaska and Hawaii became the forty-ninth and the fiftieth states.

The next time you see a funeral parade coming down Main Street of America with the flag drag coffin of a fighting warrior, be sure that your are standing tall, hand over your heart, giving a salute, or waving a American flag for this falling hero. I read a newspaper article a couple of years ago that of the twenty-first-century American men between the ages of eighteen and thirty-five, 70 percent of them are not qualified for armed services. The main reason for this sad condition is that these men have the following problems: drug-related issues, lack of education, obesity, or they just don't give a damn about our country. Our America will always need a strong military for the main purpose of homeland security reasons and for world peace. It seems that each decade, there are always conflicts and wars with very little time for peace.

According to history, most countries and kingdoms have a life span or hit their financial and military peak in about two hundred or no more than three hundred years. I am seeing some major changes in our great country that make me believe that our America has hit its peak as a financial and military world power. Also, there is a major decline in the Christian morals of our nation and there is a decreasing in changes in our business and government ethics. It's hard for me to believe what I am hearing and seeing, what has happened in the last sixty-plus years to our great America. We still want a country like that which our Founding Fathers envisioned in 1776. God can change our country only if His people start believing in our God in heaven and start praying again.

Lord Jesus, have mercy on our country as you reach down from Heaven and touch our praying hands by blessing and healing our land again. We don't want to see our America to be blowing in the wind.

3

Yes, we are still on this eighty-year-old journey of what has happened to our America. Just remember, this journey is not like that of "Let's follow the yellow gold brick road, going to see the Wizard of Oz." It's the road of where our America has been in my lifetime of eighty-plus years.

What has happened to our America that makes me believe that we are living in the end-times or last days of this church age? I don't know for sure when it all started, so I will begin with the 1960s. Get on aboard, and let's take a journey to look at where America has been and where we're going.

The main reason our Founding Fathers started public schools was that children could be taught to read their Bibles. From the founding days of our blessed country until the 1960s, the Bible, prayer, the Ten Commandments, and the Pledge of Allegiance to the Flag played a big role in our public schools. Prior to the 1960s, the biggest problems in schools were talking in class, chewing gum, and running in hallways. In my days as a grade school, junior high, and high school student, the education system of the 1940s through the 1950s, students had respect for their teachers, and teachers had respect for their students. The school principal was in control of unnecessary activity, or you were dismissed from school. Then you got a good one when you got home. Today, our schools are dealing with alcohol and drug abuse, bullying, gang activity, student sexual relationships, and violence with weapons like guns and knives. It looks like the American school system has turned into a nightmare.

It was our own US Supreme Court with the *Engel* and *Schempp* cases that changed the American education system. The results were to change religion in our public schools, that of the removal of the recitation of the Lord's Prayer and Bible reading from public schools. Because of the court decision, our schools have become the Blackboard Jungle of our education system. According to the latest survey, only 70 percent of students across the country graduate from high school. As our children go, so does our American culture. We cannot build a better-functioning America under these conditions. The question for America is, are our schools better off without God? You be the judge?

Teachers can't work under the stressful and violent conditions of today. The final result is that there will be a real big shortage of qualified teachers for the future generation of students. These times in our twenty-first century, corporate America can't find qualified or skilled workers because students are lacking knowledge in math and science. The days of the one-room schoolhouses are gone forever. Let's work together by making a better twenty-first century education system. We need to put our God back into our schools. If we don't, our education system will be just blowing in the wind. Wake up, America, before it's too late.

Again, in the 1960s, inspired by the civil rights and antiwar movement, women became more active fighting for their own rights. The fast-growing women's movement took the subject to the public. Reform came slow; few states allowed women to have abortions under certain circumstances, such as pregnancy resulting from incest and rape. In January 22, 1973, the US Supreme Court in the famous *Roe v. Wade* case, the higher court held that only a pregnant woman and her doctor have the right to make such a decision regarding abortion. The US Supreme Court declared that it could not resolve the question of when life begins. Just ask any mother or doctor, and they will tell you that human life begins at conception. From 1973 to 2015, the estimated number of cases is over 61 million abortions. Most of those years, there were over 1 million cases each year. My question to the people of America: do you want this Holocaust of America for our country? When will all this killing unborn babies come to an end?

A survey was conducted in year 2000, and found the reasons for abortion were as follows: 25.5 percent want to postpone childbearing, 21.3 percent could not afford to raise a baby; 14.1 percent, relationship with partner; 12.2 percent, young age, 10.8 percent, having baby disrupt education or job; and only 1 percent had an abortion due to rape or incest. Maybe those percentages are about the same in 2015. Many of the women who chose abortion were bullied into that decision by their boyfriends, husbands, and parents. Women who had abortion are at risk of disorders and depression, as well as committing suicide. It's time right *now* to start closing down such clinics and give such evil doctors and nurses prison time, plus make them pay high fines. The summer of 2015, we are seeing Planned Parenthood selling baby parts. Why is our federal government giving this organization half a billion dollars per year? Planned Parenthood is our nation's largest abortion provider. Also, this organization is spending unnecessary millions of dollars for party time and travel. This is our tax payers' money for their fun time.

September 2015 survey by *USA Today*/Suffolk University finds Americans back our Federal government for Planned Parenthood the use of contraception, cancer screening, and other women health services. Most Americans are most unhappy that this organization is selling baby parts for a profit to medical research.

It was a sad November 2015 day at the planned parenthood clinic in Colorado Springs, Colorado, that of shooting and killing of three people over issue of abortion. Several states are and wanting to close down these planned parenthood clinics for various reasons. These clinic issues will be in our nightly TV headlines for some time in the years to come.

Why are young kids in grade, middle, and high schools having free sex? I can't believe what has happened in our America! One of the Ten Commandments is "Thou shall not kill." What is unnecessary abortion if it is not killing?

Beware, America. God is watching our country for He has ears to hear and eyes to see what has happened to our country. Through prayers by faithful Christians, God will hear and see from heaven our crying hearts; then He will have mercy by blessing and healing our country again.

The 1960s was a period when long-held values and normal behavior seemed to be breaking down among the college-age and young people as they became political activists. Then it was the hippie movement, which was mostly middle-class young white people without any particular political drive. The hallmark was the way they dressed and their long hair. The greatest landmark was the Woodstock Festival in the year 1969, located in Upper New York State and consisted of a large crowd between 300,000 to 400,000. This large crowd celebrated days of music, love, and peace. Here in the middle of Tennessee each summer, there is the Bonnaroo Music Festival, which attracts about 85,000 people and lasts four days, with loud music and fun and good times.

The 1960s in our country were troubled times of protests, riots, and unrest situations over the Vietnam War, which lasted for many years. The US Congress authorized President Lyndon Johnson to use all necessary force after US warships came under attack in the Gulf of Tonkin. It was a war that divided our nation and left scars that are still not healed even today. Some people believed that the Vietnam War was a noble cause similar to the United Nations' efforts that kept South Korea in peace. Other people had opinions that the Vietnam War was a blunder cost with an estimated 58,000 American soldiers who lost their lives, and an estimated 153,000 fighting men wounded, and costing the taxpayers an estimated $111 billion. God Bless those American servicemen and veterans that fought for the freedom of the world—they are the true heroes of our country, and for providing the world freedom and liberty. Let freedom ring across our land, for freedom is not cheap. May God have mercy by blessing America again.

This decade was full of sorrowful times, with assassination of three great leaders of our nation: President John F. Kennedy, Dr. Martin Luther King Jr., and Senator Robert F. Kennedy. America and the rest of the world mourned the death of these three great leaders.

Our America will always, or should, remember that great speech by the thirty-fifth US president, John F. Kennedy. It was his powerful inaugural speech of January 20,1961: "Ask not what your country can do for you, ask what you can do for your country." Those were sound and powerful words from that time, and more so now in the twenty-first century.

It was Breaking News on all national and world TV stations that sad day of November 22, 1963, and for the next few days later. The world seemed to stop that day with the assassination of President John F. Kennedy while he was riding with his wife in a motorcade in Dallas, Texas. Our America and the rest of the world was saddened by the sudden death of our great and beloved president. He was buried in Arlington National Cemetery on November 25, 1963. President John F. Kennedy was selected as the 1961 Man of the Year by *Time* magazine.

One of the first things President John F. Kennedy did was create the Peace Corps, which was a great caring cause for the USA and the rest the world. The Peace Corps is a mission for people, mostly the young college-age, doing something good for mankind in this country and other countries around the world.

President Kennedy was eager for the United States to lead the way into the space age. In 1961, Alan Shepard became the first American to travel into outer space. With his approval, $2 billion was earmarked for the Project Apollo. The result from this space project was American Neil Armstrong being the first man to land on the moon, in 1969. Our America has seen both bad and good times in our space flights. Two of those space programs' brave, great people were killed either on ground or in flight. On January 1967 at Cape Kennedy, Florida, three American Apollo astronauts died in a flash fire on the spacecraft designed to take man to the moon. They were the first American spacemen to be killed on the job. These brave men were air force Lieutenant Colonel Grissom, air force Lieutenant Colonel White, and navy Lieutenant Colonel Chaffee. Progress was made in the space age. In 1981, the first space shuttle, Columbia, was launched from Cape Canaveral, Florida. Again, it was another sad day for the space program in 1986. The space shuttle Challenger blew up after liftoff, killing all six astronauts and Christa McAuliffe, a teacher to become the first civilian in space. Recall the years of the 1940s into the 1950s: comic book space heroes Flash Gordon and Buck Rogers going here and there in their spaceships. This modern age of space travel, people or spaceships are going and landing on places like Mars and the moon and then safely returning to Earth. Over seventy years ago, such space programs would never have happened, but now we are in the tomorrow space age. However, in 2014, the federal government has cut the budget for space programs.

Dr. Martin Luther King Jr. was the pastor of Dexter Avenue Baptist Church in Montgomery, Alabama. He was always a strong worker for civil rights for his church members and for his race. He directed a peaceful march in Washington DC with 250,000 people, where he delivered his famous address "I Have a Dream." This speech has encouraged our America for many years and the many years yet to come. Dr. Martin Luther King Jr. was chosen as the 1963 Man of the year for *Time* Magazine.

My fellow Americans and the future generation, what can you do for your country? And do you have a dream? don't let your dreams, hopes, and future vision be blowing in the wind.

Another shocker hit our nation in June 1968. After winning the California primary for the Democratic nomination for president of the United States, Senator Robert F. Kennedy was assassinated in Los Angles. He was the US Attorney General from January 1961 until September 1964, when he ran for the US Senate from New York State. He took office as New York state senator in January 1965.

It takes good education, faith, and hard work to be successful in this competitive business world. The faithful heroes are those who can see the invisible. The successful people of the past were seeking what was over the next hills, those mountains, and beyond the valleys. It was their vision that enabled them to see the invisible. It was the faith of our Founding Fathers that enabled them to see the invisible. They had the dreams, faith, hopes, and the vision that our America will become a greater country, for they believed in the words "God bless America" and "In God we trust." My Americans, let's put those dreams, faith, hopes, and more visions into action for this twenty-first century. As believing Christians in prayer to our God, we want our America to go forward as a Christian country again.

Now faith is being sure of what we hope for and certain of what we do not see (Heb. 11:1).

My Americans, do you have dreams and hopes of what is beyond the next mountain and beyond the valleys? You should. Our lifetime is short; be sure you don't waste your gifts, talents, and time. My Americans, let's put those God-given gifts and talents to good use today so we can have a better tomorrow for our America. This is no time to give up when you are facing hard or troubled times in your life. Just get up and start over again. Let's start up a new poster for our country: "Our America Wants You." Yes, that means *you*.

As that old saying goes, "God willing and the creek don't rise." Our God is that bridge over those troubled waters. Our country would have less financial and military problems if only the federal government just stopped raising those flood gates higher by creating more troubled waters. Some American presidents and members of Congress feel or think that a bigger federal government is better, but we all know that is not total true.

> Show me your ways, O Lord, teach me your paths;
> guide me in your truth and teach me for you are
> God my Savior, and my hope is in you all day long.
>
> —Psalm 25:4–5

4

DURING THE 1970s through the early twenty-first century, the American consumers provided the biggest surge for our country's economy. Consumer buying created more jobs as manufacturing and production increases with the demand for greater goods and services. Main Street consumers and the small business owners are the real backbone and the heartbeat for the American economy. We are really proud of our faithful and hardworking Americans. They help make this country what it should be, keeping America going forward by being more financially and militarily stronger.

The decade of the 1970s, there was a long-lasting recession of sixteen months (November 1973 through March 1975). The Organization of the Petroleum Exporting Countries (OPEC) was blamed for this recession when they quadrupled the price of oil for a few months in 1973. It was a time when people waited for hours in long lines to buy gas for their cars and trucks. Because of higher oil price, the United States went off the gold standard, and the federal government began printing more money, and the stock market took a big hit during those uncertain economic times. The Dow Jones Industrial Average dropped 45% from a peak of 1050 on January 1973 to a low of 580 by December 1974. Back in those years, oil was king of the economy world, and it still is today in this new twenty-first century.

There were major changes in Washington DC during the 1970s, with the step-down of the vice president and later with the pressure from the investigation and hearing of Watergate caused President Richard M. Nixon (1969–1974) to resign from his office. Gerald Ford became the next president of our America (1974–1977.)

Under President Jimmy Carter Administration, the years 1977 to 1981, were trouble economic times for our country. This President work hard to combat the coming woes of inflation and high unemployment, with inflation and interest rates near record highs. The final result there was a short recession in our country. Under President Carter's administration, we saw good foreign policy accomplishments with the Panama Canal Treaty and the peace treaty between Egypt and Israel.

The good news for many years was that President Carter and his wife were very active and faithful in the Habitat for Humanity program of building homes for the needy and poor people. What a God's blessing this program has become for people who can't afford housing for their family. I been financial supporting this great program for many years, you can do the same with financial support and your helping working hands by given some family their dream home. Let's work together to make happy years for these families in their new homes. May the Good Lord Bless your dream home and a big welcome to your new neighborhood.

Our nation's history during the 1980s included the last year of the Jimmy Carter presidency, eight years of the Ronald Reagan administration, and the first two years of George H. W. Bush's presidency, up to the collapse of the Soviet Union. Our America was facing uncertain times, going from financial rags to riches under these last two presidents. It was the road to recovery for our country.

President Reagan obtained approval from Congress to stimulate economic growth, control inflation, increase employment, and strengthen the national defense. The passing of both the Economy Recovery Act of 1981 and the Tax Reform Act of 1986 provided cutting taxes and simplified the income tax code. At the end of the Reagan administration, the economy was enjoying its longest recorded period in peacetime—prosperity without a recession or depression. President Reagan's great economic policies that were successful the 1980s should be applied to any recession or depression that hits our country in the future years.

The big bull market started in 1982 with the Dow Jones Industrial Average of about 700 and went on with big gains into the year 1987. The real fireworks in 1987 took place on Wall Street. The Dow Jones Industrial Average started the year at about 1900, and then made impressive advances close to 2700 with a big gain of some 44% by August that same year. What happened next was bad news on Wall Street—that is, what goes up also goes down. The fall season of 1987, Wall Street suffered the biggest decline in stock market history dropping 500 points on October 19, a decline of some 23%.

Under the Reagan administration, the passing of the Immigration Reform and Control Act of 1986 granted amnesty to illegal immigrants who entered the United States before January 1, 1982. President Reagan's goal was world peace, with such statements as, "Mr. Gorbachev, tear down this wall." The Berlin Wall came down in 1989. Overall, the Reagan years saw restoration of prosperity and the goal of world peace. He went from Hollywood movie star to governor of California and later president of America. What a great road to success for him.

The Persian Gulf War (August 1990–February 1991) under President George H.W. Bush leadership was a armed conflict between Iraq and a coalition consisting of some 46 thousand troops from thirty-two countries, lead by the United States and mandated by the United Nations. The United States began massive air attacks that destroyed much of Iraq's military capability. With these massive air strikes, Iraq and Kuwait suffered enormous property damage. Because President Saddam Hussein was not removed from power during this short war, this created the Second Persian Gulf War a few years later. The second Iraq War lasted almost ten years, plus many unknown conditions. Always be proud of our fighting warriors and the veterans, as they fought for the world's freedom and liberty.

The 1990's brought President Bill Clinton(1993-2000) who served as the 42nd President of the United States. The 1990s' economy turned into a healthy performance, as corporate earnings rose and combined with low inflation. In the year 1998, the US federal government posted its first budget surplus in almost thirty years. The 1990s was one of the best decades in years for our country. The Dow Jones Industrial Average stood just at 1000 in the late 1970s and hit just over the 11,500 mark in 1999. This put more wealth for people on Main Street America and those Wall Street investors. People across America were buying cars and trucks, homes, household goods, and they were investing both for their family future and those retirement Golden Years.

The 1980's and the 1990's under both President Ronald Reagan and President Bill Clinton were the best of economic times for our country. Americans were enjoying job growth, low inflation, and reduced taxation which enabled them to purchase whatever they needed and wanted for their lifestyle. Those were good economy times for America and the working Americans. Thank goodness for the great leadership by both the federal government and the Federal Reserve Board during those two decades, making our America greater. Yes, thank you, Lord, for blessing our America during those good years.

The first sixteen years of the new twenty-first century, our country was facing just the opposite of the 1980s–1990s' economic good times. This generation and the future generation will be seeing a lower standard of living. It will be that way for many more years to come. The big federal government of Washington DC is unable to work together as a team in handling economic conditions for our America's growth. Without good sportsmanship and teamwork, you can't win many ball games. Any future American president, his administration, and the members of Congress need to learn from those winning rules of good sportsmanship and teamwork. We need bigger changes in our business and government leadership. Our country must have good Christian leaders that have outstanding Christian ethics and good morals. My America, where are you going? Even our federal government leaders in Washington DC most of the time don't know if they are coming or going. The next midterm or national election, be sure they are going and not coming.

It's time that we put our hands to the plow and sow faith seeds in rich black soil so that those seeds will have deeper roots for our America to go forward in being financially sound and with a stronger military. It seems that our big federal government is sowing seeds in rocky soil, getting briars, thistles, and tall weeds, which in turn is creating a bankrupt country with a broken-down and confused federal government. Big federal government in Washington DC, are you hearing what Americans want from you? We don't want briars, thistles, and weeds in our daily lives. We need and want a greater America that can go forward for our children and their children. In order for our God to bless and heal our America, we must have God-fearing men and women as leaders in our local, state, and federal government. That is the only answer for our country, for God will always be with us.

America, let's stand firm and tall in what our Founding Fathers of 1776 believed in. They had dreams, hopes, and a greater vision for us. We want a country under God, with people believing in the Ten Commandments and "In God we trust." God will bless America only if Americans will please and praise our God and His Son. When we start making better changes in our Christian beliefs, morals, and ways, God will bless our country again. If we don't change our ways, there will not be a decent tomorrow for our children and their children. We will be losing all our freedoms of the press, religion, and speech. Those famous words by President Thomas Jefferson of "life, liberty, and the pursuit happiness"—those are good, strong words. Let's not forget them. Otherwise, my dear citizens of this great America, we will be seeing our America blowing in wind.

We can carry out those pursuits of happiness with our helping hands, hearts, and minds. My dear Americans, just put your God-given gifts and talents to better use, helping others in need during floods and various storms, and the hungry and starving world. President Thomas Jefferson wanted the people of this country to be serving their communities and seeking greater goodwill. We all can do this with our financial support and our helping hands.

I've been involved for almost thirty years with the Pacesetters of Cookeville, Tennessee, which is an organization for special-needs adults. What a great way of being blessed by sharing handshakes and hugs and giving your time to see to God's special-needs children, showing them that someone really cares for them. It's a double blessing for me and my special friends for we share our time together. Yes, they are God's special children, and God has a special heavenly home for them.

Let's get involved with something. Lets make our America greater. Our God wants us Christians to get more involved in His Church: being a Sunday schoolteacher, driving the church bus, working in the office, and doing janitor-yard services. Work until Jesus comes down to his church. That time of His coming for His Church is sooner than later. Always be ready and watching for His Coming.

5

It's January 1, 2000. Happy New Year, America. Welcome to the new twenty-first century. What good news and times will it bring to our country and its people? Wall Street got off to a bad start for the new century. After a strong 1990s' economy and stock market, early spring 2000 saw the walls of the stock market come crushing down. It was mostly the NASDAQ dot-com bubble stocks, with investors becoming more like spectators. They were overlooking corporate balance sheets information and the key price/earning ratios. It was impossible investments for those investors, with overvalued stocks that these companies having operative losses without turning a profit, if any, for years to come. Because of those overvalued stocks, and without any financial future for them, those dot-com companies turned into bad investments. Then there were the day traders doing online trading by buying and selling stocks through the Internet, plus many new investors were trading without any experience. It took seven years for the Dow Jones Industrial average and the S&P 500 index to break even again; the final results so many Main Street and Wall Street stock market investors took big financial losses on their investments. The NASDAQ investors had bigger financial losses on their investments, because it took fifteen long years to break even for this stock average. The final results was the big loss of several trillion dollars in the financial stock market.

Because of fear and greed, common sense may be hard to find by investing in the stock market. The days of buying stocks and holding for the long-term capital gains and yearly dividends are gone forever. At one time, it was investing in corporate America for your future years by obtaining long-term capital gains and those dividends. Now it's more like gambling because of the day traders using fast, high-tech computers. If you have any short-term capital gains, you better be selling your stock. Otherwise, because of worldwide fast economy news, your gains can be gone in minutes, or before the market even opens for trading.

September 11, 2001, was the day that changed the world, especially our America. It was the breaking news for that day and evening, with people watching the news on all major TV stations at home and around the world. Terrorists had hijacked four planes and piloted two of them into the World Trade Center's Twin Towers in New York City, and one plane crashed into the Pentagon in Washington DC. The fourth plane was on its way to the nation's capital, but the brave passengers overcame the hijackers, causing the plane to crash in a Pennsylvania field. This was the day when our country and the rest the world stood still, when almost three thousand people, including children, were killed. Americans and people around the world could not believe this had happened in our country, but it did, and we will see more of the same again in America and various places around the world.

Our country came through this uncertain time under the leadership of both New York City mayor Rudy Giuliani and American president George W. Bush. They bravely led the nation, which was facing uncertain times. Also, we are most thankful for those brave and faithful NYC firemen and policemen that came to the rescue in this great crisis. Otherwise, more people would have been killed. God bless all those families that were hurt or whose loved ones were killed during that terrible day, and he will be with them in the future. Each year on September 11, there is a time in NYC for a day in memorial of the deceased. It consists of ringing a bell after each deceased person's name is called out.

Americans across our country came together waving flags and with tears of pride for supporting the military and the president during those uncertain times. The American pride is what makes our country so great. Those brave Americans are the kind of people that are sowing seeds for the roots of our nation.

Never forget that day. It happened at Pearl Harbor and again with 9/11. Terrorists can and will strike again in America and various places around the world, so be on guard all the time. Homeland security in America and for rest of the world is here to stay. It's a costly federal government program, but it has a big purpose. That purpose is controlling and preventing future terrorist attacks in the future, saving lives and property is more important than the financial cost of this program. When you fly anytime or anywhere in the world today, it may take extra time going thru airport security; but its worth it for its your life and so many other people.

This attack of 9/11 created two wars against terrorism—they are the war in Afghanistan and the Iraq War. The war in Afghanistan began in October 2001, with the main purpose of finding Osama bin Laden and his high-ranking al-Qaeda members by destroying the organization and removing the Taliban regime. The good news is we did find him, and he was killed; but remember, there are others out there just as bad or worse than him.

The Iraq War, or Operation Iraqi Freedom, was a military campaign that began on March 2003 with the invasion led by troops from the United States and the United Kingdom. The purpose was to search for weapons of mass destruction and to overthrow Iraq's dictator, Saddam Hussein. There were no such weapons to be founded, but we did over thrown this dictator Saddam Hussein

The total financial cost for those two wars will be about $2 trillion, with additional for reconstruction costing in the billions of dollars, plus the loss of lives and the wounded of our fighting warriors. The really bad news was that most of these military men and women have been on the war front more than three to eight times. They have become mentally, physically, and spiritually worn down. When the wounded military men and women came home, these fighting warriors were not getting proper medical care from many VA hospitals across America. It became a real financial and mental hardship on them and their families back home. If these fighting heroes are good enough to fight on the battlegrounds for our freedom and liberty here in America, the federal government and the VA hospitals should be good enough to provide good medical and mental care for them and give total support for their families back home.

6

There came a man who wanted to make "Change for America." He was elected as the forty-fourth president of our country. People believed all those pipe dreams and whitewashed speeches of what he will do for your America and for you and your family. His winning the election was mainly the result of support and votes from the African American, the Mexicans, the young people, and the Encore Organization. They got their "No nonsense" wish for a change. For those last eight years of his presidency, that change did turn out what America really wanted.

The new president made his first mistake in early 2008, not hopping on top of the Great Recession that was facing our nation. He and some of his key Administration team got behind close lock doors, created the Affordable Care Act; better known as ObamaCare. At that time Democratic Speaker of the House, Nancy Pelosi, made the statement of

"Let's pass the bill so we know what is in it." That is almost like signing a housing contract: "now we can go see what our house looks like." The president, his administration team, and the Democratic-controlled Congress approved and passed the health care bill without reading it. That is like putting the cart in front of the horse. Sounds to me like they have no horse sense.

The year 2008 was the start of the "housing bust bubble," creating the Great Recession—the worst economic conditions in the last seventy years for our country. This resulted in a great stock market crash, high unemployment, and uncertain economic times. The big New York City bankers, the federal government, Fannie Mae and Freddie Mac, various mortgage companies, and the rating agency such as Moody, and Standard and Poor had misled homeowners in obtaining home loans. The final results were home foreclosures of 100,000 homes per month, with a total estimate at that time in the millions before it would hit rock bottom.

The year 2011 saw more bad news coming into the housing economy. Mortgage modification programs were not helping many homeowners that got loans restructured were winding up not able to make house payments on their mortgage again. Homeowners across America in this very depressed housing market saw home prices of national average go down 34%. Survey of late 2011 indicated that 28% of American homeowners owned more on their home than the value of their dream homes.

The effects from the Great Recession was that the average 401(k) fund took a financial hit of 33%. The stock market was hitting new highs in 2007, the Dow Jones Industrial Average was about 14,200 and the S&P 500 above 1,500. Then came the financial collapse of the year 2008. It took the Dow Jones Industrial Average and the S&P 500 seven years of breaking even.

It was not only the federal government that was having financial problems; the local and state governments across the country were too. We saw bankruptcy in our major cities like Detroit and possibly Orange County, California. The sluggish economy added more to the states' financial misery. Some states were in bad financial shape because they relied on federal stimulus programs, plus the wave of municipal defaults. Some of the states were planning or talking of selling some of their land to ease the financial strain. This is terrible for these states, as they want to sell part of our America.

During the years 2010 and beyond, our country saw many tea party and town hall gatherings where Americans were upset with the Forty-Fourth President, his administration, and the Democratic-controlled Congress. Those taxpayers and voters of America were saying to the federal government in very plain English, "We don't trust you." November 2010 midterm election, the voters got their wish for a better change by removing the Democratic-controlled House of Representatives, but the Senate was still under control, with

Senator Harry Reed and the Democratic Party. My dear Americans, let's make a better change the next time you vote in the next midterm and national election. Otherwise, we will be seeing our America blowing in the wind.

The president and his administration were having difficult times in controlling this big recession. They used all kinds of programs to stimulate the economy. There was the Cut, Cap, and Budget program so that our federal government could pay our country's bills on time. The big three programs the federal government were using to jumpstart this slow economic recovery came in the amount of $2 trillion. They were the following:

- U.S. Treasury Bond buying in amount $600 billion.
- Operation Twist in amount $400 billion.
- Trouble Assets Relief Program(TARP) in the amount one trillon dollars.

The Federal Reserve and the US Treasury working as a team of controlling the Great Recession were bailing out or pumping money into the financial system. Huge amounts of money to rescue the auto industry, the big banks. Also, organizations such as AIG, Freddie Mac, and Fannie Mae were saved from drowning in their own debts.

Mainly due to lack of faithful leadership and lack of good old-fashioned business experience, we were seeing many business and government leaders of our America lacking business ethics, and they have gotten greedier. This must come to a fast stop for our children and their children. We want more Christian men and women as faithful leaders in our local, state, and federal government, so we can move forward toward becoming a greater and a stronger America.

At last we were seeing recovery from the Great Recession. The Federal Reserve Board with the Secretary of the Treasury had done an excellent job bringing the economy back alive for America and that of the world economy. The Federal Reserve Board had kept inflation under control. As of December 2014, inflation was low at 0.8%. By December 2015, inflation came in with low reading of 1.5 %, forecast is about 2% for end of 2016, which is still very low.

At last on December 2015, the Federal Reserve Board raised short term interest rates for the first time in nearly ten years. Fed Chairlady Janet Yellen stated that it will be several years before interest rates be back to normal, which is closer to 4 percent if the US economy is forming well. This increase of rates had been a big concern for several months on Wall Street with those big-time stock investors. At their March and June 2016 monthly meeting, the Fed had no plans to change short-term interest rates in the near future; there have been forecasts of maybe one or two more rate increases for rest of year 2016. These should be baby steps increases. The Fed's job is to protect against inflation while maintaining full employment for our country. Such an interest rate increase will be the end of easy money for borrowing and lending. The borrowing rates will rise; the banks tend to be slow in raising saving rates and quick to increase borrowing rates.

The main reason for this delay of raising rates by the Federal Reserve Board is as following:

There were major concerns due to China's slower economy, very uncertain global stock market, and the strong dollar facing America's economy. Also, they were waiting for improvement in the job market, which turn out the employment rate dropped to 5 percent by end of December 2015.

The Gross National Product (GNP) is the value of goods and services produced in the USA. The final reading for the GNP was 2.4 per cent for the year ended 2015. During the year 2015 there were lots of ups and downs affecting the GNP for each quarter. The economy was down in the first quarter mostly due to the following reasons: very cold weather with big snow in the Midwest and Northeastern states, the strong American dollar, and the port labor strike on the West Coast. The second quarter of 2015 came in stronger with consumer spending and home construction. The third quarter came in with weaker export sales due to stronger dollar. The last quarter was much weaker of 0.7 GNP than was forecast which was due to these conditions: business and consumers spend less money, plus the trade gap had widened, and a much weaker global stock market. The only good news for the final quarter 2015 was a stronger job market, that average 284,000 per month. The forecast by leading economist for year 2016 about 2.0 GNP, it might be closer to 2.5 for the GNP; that is if the America's economy engines are running in overdrive or being more supercharge.

Just look back few years ago, the Dow Jones Industrial average was 1,000 (December 1972) and at 10,000 (March 1999). Let take a closer look at the Dow Jones Industrial average, the S&P 500 index, and the Transportation average of the past three years of 2013, 2014, and 2015, showing the closing low, closing high, and the year-end closing.

	DOW INDUSTRIAL average	S&P 500 INDEX	TRANSPORTATION
FOR YEAR 2013			
LOW	13,000	1,400	5,300
HIGH	16,600	1,900	7,400
CLOSING	16,600	1,900	7,400
FOR YEAR 2014			
LOW	15,400	1,700	7,100
HIGH	18,000	2,100	9,200
CLOSING	17,800	2,100	9,100
FOR YEAR 2015			
LOW	15,700	1,900	7,500
HIGH	18,300	2,100	9,200
CLOSING	17,400	2,000	7,500

According to the STOCK TRADER ALAMAX the months of November, December, and January are the best 3 months of the year for the Main and Wall Street investors. Not so in the last two months of 2015 and the month January 2016. The Santa Claus Rally which covers the final 5 trading days of 2015 and the first 2 trading sessions of January 2016 did not taken place this time. When Santa rally pan out, look out for bad news on Wall Street. The month of January 2016 got off the worst start ever in American stock market history. The first 3 weeks of January 2016, the Dow Industrial average was down to 15,800, the S&P 500 index was down to 1,900, and the Transportation average was down to 6,600; these were big time losses for stock market investors. The month of February on the average is also down month for the stock market, after the first two weeks this proved to be true. Market corrections as this one, there is always lots of fear and panic as investors seeing their retirement shrink. The Federal Reserve Board chairlady did not help matters at all during the February 2016 meeting without any positive news The main reasons for such a big decline in the stock market in the first two months of 2016 was mostly due to slower China economy, bigger dropped in WTI crude oil prices, new fear of American economy, and a stronger US dollar. The American corporations in the S&P 500 index were seeing their sales/profit lower due to surging US dollar, because great deal of those sales come from Asia and Europe. When the dollar rises against the yen and the euro, America made products become more expensive to customers in those countries.

Various surveys show on an average a correction of 5 per cent every two or three months, a 10 per cent decline once a year, and a big 20 per cent bear market downturn about three or five years; so be aware of such corrections for its your hard earned money. Since 1900 there has been 35 bear markets, decline of 20 per cent or more. The great investor, Warren Buffet has the best answer for investing in the stock market. His famous motto is "Be fearful when others are greedy and be greedy while others are fearful." Again, another of his wise investment motto is "You want to learn from experience, but you want to learn from other people's experience when you can."That ole says "The roses will bloom again," is the same with investing in the stock market for the market will bottom out and in time will reach new highs again. By mid- April 2016 the American stock market was heading much stronger upward as positive news start coming in such as the following: The Federal Reserve Board is on hold, rising oil prices, and a weaker US dollar. Also, America's leading corporate CEO's are more upbeat for the second half of 2016 and beyond into year 2017 for economic improvement. However, beware of any news from the Fed regarding future interest rate increases, the folks on Wall Street don't like those unknown kind of news. Just remember that we are living in a world economy, what happens in others countries like China and the PIIGS can affect world markets for some time.

In Europe they are known as the PIIGS countries consisting of following: Portugal, Ireland, Italy, Greece, and Spain. They were the ones having their own budget financial crisis and default on their debts. Until the European debt crisis is solved, there will be more stock market volatility around the world.

June 2016 with a surprise decision Britain (UK), voted to leave the European Union (EU). This created a big global stock market crashed where stocks went down between 4 per cent to over 12 per cent, WTI crude oil tumbled 5 per cent, and the British pound sterling dropped to 10 per cent to a 31year low vs the dollar. This all took place in just one trading day. Even on the second trading day global stock market were down big time. The Dow Industrial average and the S&P500 were down over 5 per cent for those two days of trading. Out of the 28 countries in the EU, Britain was the first country to dropped out, maybe the only one after this bloodbath. The good news, the global stock market heading up.

In the last couple years, we have seen the price of West Texas Intermediate (WTI) crude oil go from $107 per barrel to low $26.20 as of February 2016. Many of those smaller and mid-size gas/oil companies in Alaska, North Dakota, Oklahoma, and Texas may be forced into mergers in order to keep their business being more financial sound, some might be forced into being bankrupt. The big giant gas/oil companies like Chevron, ConocoPhillips, and ExxonMobil will be okay, but will have lower sales/profit for some time. They all have to wait much longer for that $50 to $100 WTI crude oil prices per barrel again. In the meantime, there will be many employee layoffs, the federal and state government will be receiving less incoming taxes from those gas/oil companies. Also, there will be a major financial hardship to those families and business places that are located in those affected cities and towns. The price of WTI crude oil might be between $45 to $50 per barrel by Labor Day week end 2016 or much higher going into 2017. The price of unleaded regular gas in my hometown of Cookeville, Tennessee hit a low of $1.45 per gallon and the national average of $1.70 as of February 2016. By July 2016 unleaded regular gas is higher of about $2.10 per gallon national average, this is because of higher oil prices over $40 per barrel. Price in my hometown of Cookeville for regular gas is $1.80 per gallon. It may go lower as the summer driving season comes to an end after Labor Day weekend 2016. This is still cheap for gas comparing to past years of $3 to about $4 per gallon. This is will be good news as consumers be hitting the roads for their week end trips and those summer vacations.

The same with the cost of natural gas, because of a mild 2015/2016 winter the cost of natural gas was about $2 BTU. Even in very cold winters of past years, the price of natural gas had reached between $3 to $4 BTU. As hot summer months coming ahead of us, the price of natural gas will be heading higher. The main reason there are more utility companies now than ever before that rely on natural gas to generate electric power instead that of coal because it is cleaner and cheaper.

What cause this big decrease in West Texas Intermediate (WTI) crude oil prices is the old game of supply and demand. It will be depended on the oil producing countries such as OPEC, Russia, and the United States of their production demands. Even a big conflict between Iran and Israel can set off a big jump in oil prices. Our own president wants a $10 per barrel oil tax. This new oil tax would be phased in over the next five years and would have bad financial affect to both domestic and import oil. The following are some reasons for that larger oil supply:

- Domestic production surge due to fracking.
- OPEC did not decrease production of oil.
- Less oil consumed in America and other countries.
- Americans driving less and having better car/truck gas mileage.

One of the really bad concerns facing America is that fewer people are saving for their golden retirement years. A study shows that only 36% of Americans have nothing saved. The result is that 26% of those fifty- to sixty-four-year-olds haven't saved a thing for their golden years, while those young people of eighteen to twenty-nine years old saved nothing. This will be a really big problem in the future for the American economy and a big headache for Uncle Sam.

The so-called baby boomers (born 1946–1964) are turning sixty-five years old at the rate of ten thousand people per day. People are living longer because of better medical care and scientific and medical research. This is what people like and want if they are in good health. An American born today has a projected average life span twenty years longer than one born ninety years ago; that is comparing the age of fifty-nine to age seventy-nine for today. According to the Congressional Budget Office as of May 2015, one-fifth of the US population will be sixty-five years old or older, up from 12% in year 2000. As the baby boomers grow older, will their children, known as the millennial generation, be able to take care of them? This new generation of the millennials, which is about 80 million strong, will not have the same standard of living as their parents. There may be a real hardship on both generations. As each year rolls around, there will be a bigger demand for more federal government programs such as Medicare and Social Security to take care of these older people. Will this have a positive or a negative effect on the future America's economy and maybe that of your lifestyle? What do you think?

After the Great Recession of 2007 to 2011, it was a long hill to climb up for the construction industry. During those hard times of that recession, 2.3 million construction workers lost their jobs. The good news start coming back in the Spring and Summer months of 2015, as the housing industry start to recovery for both new apartment buildings and for family homes. However, during the last half of 2015 and going into the months of 2016, there is still a shortage of skilled construction workers. These are people such as carpenters, roofers, and construction operators; and that due to higher housing materials as production play catch up. Majority of home buyers want to live in or near cities, that land for home building is becoming more expensive.

Home builders were having problems finding land to buy for home building for there is less land for development. I am seeing some home builders in my hometown are building smaller condos and homes without garages because of shortage of development and expensive land. The housing industry is an important key for a healthy economy that provides middle wage jobs for builders, craftmen, and supplier of building materials. As of April 2016, home mortgage rates are still very reasonable between 3.75 to 4.0 per cent. These are good housing news or signs for the whole America's economy for the year 2016 and many future years to come. According to a June 2016 report that existing home sales for that month were hitting higher sales, the best in the last nine years.

7

THE LAST TWENTY or more years, I have enjoyed reading the Bible prophecy. I believe that we are living more than ever in the end-times or the last days of this church age. What is this I am reading in the daily newspaper, or hearing and seeing on the evening TV news regarding America and world events? What will really happen to our America and the world in the years to come, just read your Bible each day for all the answers.

We are seeing the deteriorating moral and ethical values in our country, plus the downfall of America. These are some of those signs: more abortion, abuse of children and women, alcohol and drug addiction, divorces, and an increase in violent crimes. Also, the new twenty-first century finds the whole world being plagued with terrorism and the political tension from oil-related countries. The life span for a counry or nation is about two hundred to three hundred years before it hits its financial and military peak as a world power nation. This has happened during the twentieth century and more so in the new twenty-first century, that our own America is losing its financial world power and military strength. America is still the leader in world economy, with China at a close second place. However, in the years to come that may change as China's GNP is growing much faster than that of the United States. It's sad that our great America is bankrupt with a nation debt almost $20 trillion by sometime the year 2017 and going more debt each year, plus paying high interest on that borrowed money. Since 1962, the national debt ceiling has been raised each year. We must not be raising the national debt ceiling each year, in order for the federal government to be spending and wasting more money. Our federal government must stop printing more money and stop borrowing almost 45 cents for each dollar spent. The time is coming when our America will be faced with higher inflation, interest rates, and taxes. Otherwise, if our country doesn't change their greedy and selfish ways and don't control the federal budget, you will be seeing your America, blowing in the Wind.

Most Americans were feeling uneasy with their lower standard of living. According to a Fox TV News survey, as of August 2014, that 71 percent of Americans feel that our America is on the wrong financial track. Also, the Federal Reserve survey of August 2014 indicated that 25 percent of families were just getting by, living one week one paycheck at a time to the next week. More bad news is that about 50 million Americans are living in poverty, just living on food stamps and having part-time jobs. This also includes the homeless and our military fighting warriors and their family. Most Americans in this new twenty-first century feel that their children and grand children will not enjoy the same standard of living as they are. According to a 2012 poll by Scott Rasmussen, that older American parents feel this way regarding their standard of living.

We are hearing too many lies from the White House and the House of Congress, that most Americans are fed up with the federal government. The years the Forty-Fourth President have been in office, Americans are seeing many scandals without any results being solved. These are just a few of them:

- Passing Affordable Care Act, better known as ObamaCare, without reading it.
- Four Americans were killed by terrorists on September 2011 in Benghazi, Syria, just before the 2012 national election, which was ignored by the president till after the election and still unsolved as of 2015.
- Call girls in South America involved with Secret Services while protecting the US president.

- The IRS targeting conservative groups prior to the national election of 2012.
- Lack of medical care for veterans in VA hospitals.
- Illegal migrants crossing the border from Central America and Mexico into America, many of them students heading to our schools.
- Release of detainees, plus the five most dangerous ones from Guantanamo Bay.
- ISIS terrorists in Iraq and Syria beheading people.
- The issue of same-sex marriage rights.
- Fraud with the food stamp program.
- Lack of control of cyber hackers.
- Uncertainty over nuclear weapons deal with Iran.

All the above scandals just got out of hand, with the big federal government in Washington DC having no solutions to address the above conditions. The Forty-Fourth President made a statement back in the year 2008 when he took office "I like being president, for I can do anything I want." My dear faithful Americans, this does not sound like a faithful president; rather, it sounds like an unfaithful ruler.

As of late November 2014, the president signed an executive order to protect 5 million undocumented immigrants from deportation, allowing foreign workers trained in high technology fields to enter and stay in our country. This president was bypassing the US Congress and ignoring the US Constitution. Because of this action, the Forty-Fourth President had received more resistance than support. According to a *USA Today* poll, 64 percent of the people say he should wait for the new Republican-controlled Congress to act on this issue.

When the Founding Fathers wrote the Constitution, they separated the power to write the law from the power to execute the law in order to protect the liberties of the American people. They did this knowing that putting too much power in a single branch of government would lead to tyranny. The Constitution is clear that it is Congress's job to write the laws and the president's to enforce them. This Forty-Fourth President or any future presidents from both parties must not be allowed to ignore the US Constitution and bypassing the US Congress at any time of writing and passing new laws for our country.

Most Americans did not like the release of five of the most dangerous detainees in exchange for one deserter US Army soldier named Sergeant Bowe Bergdhal. The debate is, should he spend years or a life sentence in prison as punishment for endangering other soldiers who risked their lives to find him? Sometime in 2016, Sgt. Bowe Bergdhal will be sentence as a deserter by the US Army Martial Law Court system. How will the Forty-Fourth President handle this case before leaving office in January 2017? A few years ago, this president made this US Army deserter look like a hero with Bergdhal's parents on national TV. Then there is the release of many detainees from Guantanamo Bay, which they went to fight for the ISIS terrorists to attack both Iraq and Syria; they joined up with the ISIS as terrorist fighters.

The issue of same-sex marriage rights was voted in by the US Supreme Court as of June 2015. It was a 5–4 decision by the higher court of having same-sex marriage across all fifty states. Democrats cheer the decision for civil rights. The higher court voted for what the Forty-Fourth President wanted, not for what is best in God's eyes. By the request of the president, the White House was lifted up in rainbow colors to celebrate Supreme Court decision on same sex marriage. The majority of Americans want the higher court to make the final decision. According to an April 2015 write-up in *USA Today*, a poll shows that 60 percent of the age group of eighteen to thirty-four support gay marriage, while from the older people, those over age sixty-five, only 40 percent support same-sex marriage. While 60 percent of Americans oppose, a law would allow people to refuse business services to a same-sex wedding. In the year 2003, there was only one state that allowed same sex marriage; as of May 2015, there are thirty-seven states, plus the District of Columbia, where gay marriage is legal.

Kim Davis, county clerk of Rowan, Kentucky, went to jail over the Labor Day weekend of five days by the order of a federal district judge for her Christian beliefs of not marrying same sex couples. God bless you, my dear Christian lady. There should been more county clerks across our America to stand up and back up Kim Davis for her beliefs. Because of the Supreme Court ruling on same sex marriage, this may be the beginning of targeting churches, Christian business owners, and Christian colleges.

With about the 50 million people in America who are on food stamps, report came out on Fox News as of February 2015 that there is a big fraud in this program. The amount of money from this food stamp program fraud came to $858 million. There is talk on Capitol Hill in Washington DC to have a law of showing ID cards before receiving food stamps. This food stamp program should be used only for the purchase of food, not sold for cash so people could be buying alcoholic drinks and drugs.

As of December 2014, the FBI has confirmed that North Korea is behind the latest cyber attacks. If this ever happened in our country, our America would be out of electric power, and people would lose all their financial-medical records. This in turn would create another great recession, causing a worldwide stock market crash. As of May 2015, there is an agreement between China and Russia that they will not carry out cyber attacks against each other. Our federal government has been blaming them for hacking our computers.

We have seen this in our America in the past year or so: cyber hackers were stealing people's records showing names, addresses, phone numbers, and social security numbers. They were hitting retail store corporations like Target just before the holiday season of 2013, affecting an estimate of 40 million customers. The fall season of 2014, hackers were hitting both Home Depot and Michaels customers. February 2015, hackers were stealing customers' records from health care insurer Anthem of 80 million people. May 2015, 104,000 taxpayers had personal information stolen from the IRS by hackers. Again, in June 2015, hackers got into the records of over 4 million US federal records. In time hackers from other counties will steal highly secrets from our federal government. Maybe they already have. Our government blamed China, but they said it was not true. There will be others in the future. During these end-times days, crazy or dishonest hackers can and will wipe out your lifetime savings and other records of importance such as Medicare and Social Security. In time, hackers from other countries like China and Russia will get into our US military plans and records, and there will be no more top military secretes in Washington DC.

As of December 2014, the Forty-Fourth President made an agreement with Cuba, lifting embargo for future trade with the world. After fifty years under the control of the

Castro brothers, it was good news for the Cuban people, which will lead to greater freedom and liberty for them. Also, it provides a better standard of living for the people of Cuba in the years to come. In April 2015, the Forty-Fourth President told Congress that he has plans to remove Cuba from the US terrorism list and to allow expanded travel and trade opportunities. This should make for better trade relationship between the USA and that island plus other countries around the world. Now the Cuban flag is flying at the embassy in Washington for the first time in fifty years. After almost eighty-eight years as of March 2016, the American President made a short visit to Cuba. The Forty-Fourth President had plans to focus on rebuilding commercial ties between the USA and Cuba plus draw a better relationship with the Castro government.

The Forty-Fourth President, after visiting Knoxville, Tennessee, in January 2015 wants to use the same idea as Tennessee of having free two-year community college education for the whole country. The federal government would pay 75 percent of the cost while each state would make up for the difference. The students would be responsible for their own education, earn good grades, and stay on for their degree. The president did not say at that time how this free two-year community colleges would be financed or paid by the government. It should be a good program for creating better and more jobs for America as Americans become better educated.

Over the past few years, the Forty-Fourth President ignored the voices of America. When the Americans went to vote in November 2014, it was a big victory win for the Republican Party. The GOP took complete control of Congress by winning a majority in the US Senate and electing the largest GOP majority in the US House; plus they captured more state governors and state legislators. It looks like the Grand Old Party is laying the groundwork for moving into the White House after the November 2016 national election.

Late December 2014, this was a warning from this controlling Forty-Fourth President to congressional Republicans: "I have a veto pen and come January 1, 2015, I won't be afraid to use it." Yes, the Forty-Fourth President did used that ink pen plus a big bottle of ink as he made many vetoes during 2015 without Congress approval. There will be many more vetoes before this president be leaving office by January 2017. Wake up, my American citizens and people in Washington, DC, on Capitol Hill, of what has happened to our USA.

Senate GOP majority political members are hoping to have plans to derail president plans on climate change, health care, and immigration. It looks like a big, nasty dogfight between the Forty-Fourth President and both Senate Majority Leader Mitch McConnell and the Speaker of the House John Boehner and now new Speaker of the House Paul Ryan. The president needs to dig his heels into action of working as a team with Congress and getting our America on the right road to success.

In January 2015, the US House and the Senate passed the Keystone XL Pipeline Bill; and the Forty-Fourth President got his veto pen out to use, with full ink bottle and the blotter, and the last week of February, he turned down the bill. With millions of Americans out of work and millions more working part-time because they can't find full-time jobs, this should have been top priority for the Forty-Fourth President, to work together with both his administration and Congress. This pipeline project would have brought in billions of dollars of revenue to the local, state, and federal governments. The Forty-Fourth President was not looking at better jobs for America, but was more concerned with environmental concerns. Transportation of this oil by pipeline would be lot safer for environmental issues than that by using either highway trucking or the railroad. The chances of any overruled by the US Congress over the Forty-Fourth President's veto may be very small or none at all. In November 2015, the president says no to the Keystone XL Pipeline project from Canada. He feels the project doesn't serve USA's national interest as the six-year review comes to a close, stating, "So while our polities have been consumed by debate over whether or not this pipeline would create jobs and lower gas prices, we have gone ahead and created jobs and lowered gas prices." This president had created bad feelings with Canada for his decision. He is not looking to the future for our country. The next USA president may have different ideas regarding to this pipeline project, for it would create about forty-two thousand well-paying temporary jobs over two years.

The federal government, through the Department of Transportation, will be making it harder on freight tanker car trains. By year 2019, about 30,000 older tankers will be replaced or upgraded with thicker steel to reduce derailments. In past years lots of accidents with fiery explosions and people being killed from such derailments.

On September 2015, ISIS terrorists were on a murderous rampage of killing 129 and wounding 350 people in Paris, France. President Hollande of France declared a state of emergency and closed borders. It was the worst and deadliest violent attack since World War II for that country. The French government maintained its highest terrorist alert system for the possibility of another attack. A few days later, a historic crowd of more than a million people, including 40 world leaders, jammed the streets in Paris expressing their feelings against ISIS terrorism and paying homage to the victims on the attack of their beloved city. Who was missing as a world leader in Paris? Yes, it was our president, vice president, and secretary of state for that big *why*. That same morning before the attack, our Forty-Fourth President stated that ISIS was now contained. Mr. President, you were wrong again.

Who was missing from the United States as one of the world leaders in this rally: the Forty-Fourth President, the vice president, and the secretary of state were not there. WHY? This doesn't look good for our America, when our *big* federal government leaders are looking so *little*.

In January 2015, the Forty-Fourth President gave his sixth State of the Union Address from Congress on national TV. He spoke of his plans for the next two years for our country. His proposals would raise taxes of $320 billion for the next ten years on the wealthy. This would help pay the cost of $175 billion of tax credits to the middle-class families. Also, they would pay the $60 billion for college education. These plans are as followed:

- Raised taxes by $320 billion for the wealthy American over the next ten years.
- Raised top capital gains tax rate from 23.8% to 28% on the wealthy.
- Tax credit up to $500 for the two-earner filers with income up to $120,000.
- Child care credit up to $3,000 for families with income up to $120,000.
- Tax credit for college students up to $2,500 a year for five years.

In this State of the Union Address, the president announced that he wants to increase the minimum wage to $10.10 from the present $7.25. Also, requiring employers to provide paid sick leave and parental leave for their employees. The latest poll as of February 2015, most Americans agree with the Forty-Fourth President. However, this same AP-GfK poll shows that most Americans don't approve of how the president is helping the middle class. Fast food workers are getting ready for their biggest strike on Tuesday November 10, 2015. The group representing the workers fight for $15 an hour, to protests against restaurants in 270 cities across America. This is the most protests since it began organizing the demonstration three years ago. Over the next year, the walkout will be on November 10, exactly twelve months before to the national election. This group plans to organize as many as 64 million Americans who earn less than $15 an hour to register and vote. Look out for any presidential candidate in favor of a $15 minimum wage and for worker's right to unionize. This might have a major effect on the 2016 election of who will be getting the most votes.

After few years of employee protests and outrage over their low pay, Walmart, as of April 2015, will start providing raises of $9 per hour or more to their 500,000 low-paid workers. By February 2016, hourly workers will make at lease $10 per hour after completing six months of training. Our country saw other wage demonstrations by fast food workers demanding higher wages. The fast-food restaurants are following the same wage increases sometime in the spring or summer, not the $15 per hour as some workers demanded. As of February 2015, twenty-nine states and DC have minimum wages above $7.25, ranging from $7.50 to $9.50 per hour.

The eight years of the Forty-Fourth President's administration, with both the House and the Senate, resulted in the least productive legislative era that may be on record. With the results of the 2014 national election, with the GOP in control of both the House and Senate, that should change after the 2016 national election. We need and want a US president that will work with both parties in Congress. Those eight years in office the Forty-Fourth President always had a full bottle of black ink for his veto pen. When it comes to signing the national budget, this president should be using red ink pen because our country is in debt of 19 billion dollars going into the year 2016.

It is time to stop this backstabbing, finger pointing, and blaming each party for this and that. We must work together as a team so we can have a winning country. Because if our confusing big, fat federal government in Washington DC will not change, God will turn His back on America; maybe He has already done that. No more of this kicking the can down the road. The taxpayers and voters of America need to be kicking the fat lazy cans of the political people on Capitol Hill down the road.

March 3, 2015, Israel's prime minister, Benjamin Netanyahu, addressed the U.S. Congress, explaining the many dangers from Iran's powerful nuclear program. The PM feels any deals with Iran would not work the best for

Israel, because they don't trust Iran and their leaders. This will be his third address; the first one was back in 1996 three weeks after his election as Israel's PM. Missing from his address was the Forty-Fourth President, the Vice President, and various members of their Democratic Administration. There has been many conflicts over the years between our Forty-Fourth President and Israel's prime minister. The Forty-Fourth President claims that their meeting is too close to Israel's election in March 17, 2015. The Forty-Fourth President of the USA has forgotten again that Israel is God's Holy Land and that the people of Israel are holy people.

Prime Minister Benjamin Netanyahu of Israel won easy for the fourth time. He does not want his country to be split with any other country. However, the Forty-Fourth President does not agree with that decision.

There is a big disagreement between the Forty-Fourth President and the PM regarding a nuclear deal with Iran. The prime minister of Israel claims that any unfavorable deal will be a dream deal for Iran and a nightmare deal for the rest of the world. The PM demands a stronger deal that ensures Iran will not develop a nuclear bomb in secret. I feel that the PM is right for he knows for sure what lies ahead for Israel, that Iran is in his backyard. What the future holds is a big unknown question between our Forty-Fourth President and Israel's PM.

In mid-April 2015, the six World Power countries—of Britain, China, France, Germany, Russia, and the USA—were still working out a comprehensive deal with Iran over nuclear weapons. Iran's president claims it will be a difficult path for their country to reach a final peaceful deal. As of late July into early August 2015, our secretary of state, John Kerry, came up with a fast agreement with Iran. It looks like our Forty-Fourth President wants anything good or bad, just as long he gets an agreement. Most Americans do not like this deal with Iran, including many Democrats.

Israel's top representatives believe the Iran nuclear deal was a dangerous misstep. Majority of Congress is against the deal. Will they have enough votes to override presidential veto, is the big question. It looks like the PM of Israel knows what lies ahead for his country of any unknown nuclear weapons deals with Iran more than the Super Six countries and the Forty-Fourth President.

Over the years, there has been many world leaders who have addressed our US Congress. The following are some of them: British PM Margaret Thatcher in 1985, Great Britain Queen Elizabeth II in 1991, Russian president Boris Yeltsin in 1992, South African leader Nelson Mandela in both 1990 and 1994, British prime minister Tony Blair in 2003, and German chancellor Angela Merkel in 2009, plus other world leaders over the years. At this time in our uncertain world, the prime minister of Israel was a good and wise choice to address our US Congress.

It was fifty years ago, March 1965, when the march from Selma to Montgomery, Alabama, took place. State troopers attacked demonstrators protesting discriminatory practices that kept black voters from the polls. They had gathered at the Edmund Pettus Bridge in Selma that year for the fifty-four-mile journey to the state capital in Montgomery. There were 600 peaceful protesters that were brutally attacked by law enforcement armed with billy clubs and tear gas who became known as Bloody Sunday. About two weeks later, Dr. Martin Luther King Jr. led a march to the state capital under federal protection by the order of President Lyndon Johnson. Later that year, President Johnson signed the Voting Rights Act for the black people's right to vote.

Fifty years later, people gathered by the thousands at that famous bridge in Selma, Alabama, for the fiftieth anniversary of March 1965. Even the Forty-Fourth President of America gave a speech in Selma that weekend. Lots of changes have been made and seen from the time President Lincoln gave freedom to slaves 150 years ago to that time of Selma 1965, and now of the new twenty-first-century March 2015.

However, there are still racial tensions across our country, the following are just some of them. August 2014, the incident of the shooting of an unarmed black teenager by white police officer in Ferguson, Missouri. Later at his trail, the police officer was founded to be not guilty, which created more tension in that city of Ferguson. Then there was the case in North Charleston, South Carolina where a white police officer was charged with murder (shoot eight time)of unarmed black man. Again, April 2015 in Baltimore, Maryland where police officers arrested a black man who died in police squad van. After two weeks of protests and riots, the local police and 3,000 National Guard was enforcing night time curfew. Baltimore's top prosecutor had filed criminal charges of second degree murder and involuntary manslaughter against all six police officers for failure to render medical aid to this black man who suffered from fatal spinal injury while in police custody. There are so many cases like these in the past few years in this country. The big question is how, when, and where will all these protesting, riots, shooting/killings ever end? The only answer, it will take lots of prayers as the city leaders and church pastors come together with the love of Jesus for total peace.

As I am writing this book, May 10, 2015, it's Mother's Day. Being a housewife and a mother must be the hardest and most rewarding job there is. There was this black Hero Mother that was concerned about her teenage son who was there during the riots in Baltimore. She was not going to allow her teenage son to be just another punk in the streets looking for trouble. She was compelling him come home instead of throwing rocks at police officers . God Bless all you, Mothers across our land, for showing your care and love for your children.

The love of American mothers for their children is being seen across our land. As of May 2015, the Million Moms March was sponsored by Mothers for Justice United, an organization of mothers whose children have been killed by police officers. They march in Washington DC from the US Capitol to the Department of Justice as the crowd shouted, "No Justice, No Compromise!"

The summer of 2015, a white man opened fire during a prayer meeting inside a historic black church, the Emanuel AME Church in Charleston, South Carolina. It was a hate crime, killing nine people, including the pastor, who was the state senator. In a time like this, of senseless and crazy shootings and killings, we must turn to God for a healing of our faith and to our mind. We must stand on our beliefs and faith that we are on the race of Americans. The governor of South Carolina stated, "It's time to take down the Confederate flag from the state house." There were mixed feelings in our nation over the removal of this flag.

Our country has seen several shooing and killing at high schools and colleges over the years. In October 2015, a gunman killed nine Christians and wounded several students at Umpqua Community College, Roseburg, Oregon. This God-hating gunman ordered students to stand up and state if they were Christians. As they stood up, the shooter said: "Good, because you are a Christian, you will be seeing God in just about one second." He shot them in the head for their belief. As Christians, we must prepare our self for persecution. Christ strongly warned Christians that to follow Him would not be popular.

In fact, everyone who wants to live a godly life in Christ Jesus will be persecuted (2 Timothy 3:12).

Over the years of this twenty-first century, our country has seen many shootings and killings at several college and university campuses. Also, seeing many racial protesting and discrimination incidents of students across college campuses, like that at the University of Missouri in November 2015. My question to America, What has happened to our colleges and universities in the last fifty-five-plus years? It has gotten out of hand since I was a college student when I graduated from Ball State University the class of 1960.

The Forty-Fourth President is attacking the NRA and wanting tighter gun laws. Mr. President it's not the gun that is doing the shooting, it's the mad gunman. The idea of gun-free zones is not the answer that being against any crazy mad gunman; for they are the ones that go such places for these shootings and killings. Dr. Ben Carson, the GOP 2016 presidential candidate, has the right answer, that of expanding efforts to identify and treat the mentally ill person before they commit any acts of violence.

In May 2015, the Justice Department announced that it will provided $20 million to police departments for body cameras. This will become a three-year program with a budget of $70 million. Because of so many terrorism and violence attacks in our country and rest of the world, we need better and more training programs for both our firemen and police officers. During these trouble times in our country, we are hearing and seeing on national TV that of "Kill a Cop" for no reason. During the summer months of 2016, we have seen several shooting/killing of police officers and there seems to be no end of these violent shooting/killings. Such cases as in Baton Rouge killing three police officers and that of Dallas killing five police offices and wounded seven others in a matter of a week apart. This must STOP NOW. It may come a time in our country when local and state government will have to pay hazard duty pay for these brave police officers. Take time to thank these brave firemen and police officers in your community and towns with a good hand shake or a pat on the back. They are on the job twenty-four hours each day to protect you and your family all the time.

There are so much hatred for Christians in our country and rest of the world. None of us know what the future holds; the hatred toward the name of Jesus and Christianity will continue. Believers in the Middle East countries are dying because of their faith. ISIS terrorist are beheading Christians by the hundreds. We are seeing in Israel as of October 2015, killers are saying, "Kill a Jew." These God haters are doing this killing with a knife.

The churches in Ferguson, Missouri and St. Louis county plus the cities of Baltimore, Maryland and Miami need to come together in prayer with the love and peace for all the families that lived across our America. Thank goodness the Billy Graham Evangelistic Association had sent chaplains as a support group to bring the love of Christ to the people of Ferguson and St. Louis County. When the Gospel goes into these areas of chaos and hurt, it opens the doors to people's hearts to receive our Lord Jesus. It will take the love of Jesus Christ to bring total peace from all these riots, shooting, and killings. As Christians, we need to stand up and speak up for our biblical values and turn to God, for He has all the answers of any problems that are facing our country.

President Thomas Jefferson said, "The best government is that which governs least." It's a crying shame that the politicians in Washington DC in this twenty-first century don't have the wisdom of our Founding Fathers. Mr. President and members of Congress's bigger government is not better government.

The US Postal Service is heading toward a financial fallout, posting a huge $5.5 billion loss in the fiscal year 2014. This is eight years in a row of billion-dollar losses. Also, adding to the financial problem, the PS is in the process of spending $5.5 billion for the purchase of 180,000 new trucks. They are moving into one-day postal services and grocery delivery services, hoping to offset some of the losses. There are plans that the postal services might be using drones for their mail delivery. Our country cannot do without the postal services for it is a must for business and for Americans to receive their mail. The final result in the next few years is that there will be a bailout paid by the American taxpayers. Our mailing system has come a long way from the days of the Pony Express and that of the stagecoach. Now in our twenty-first century, we are seeing faster and cheaper mail services by e-mail through the Internet. What the future holds for the US Post Office is still a big unknown from all their financial problems that have been facing them over the years.

Let's be proud of our America. We have come a long way in the last four hundred years from the Pilgrims of the 1600s crossing the Atlantic Ocean to come to the New World, the early settlers forming the thirteen colonies, the Founding Fathers of 1776 signing the laws for our freedom and liberty. The 1800s, there was freedom from slavery and the pioneers heading westward across America to the West Coast. During the twentieth and twenty-first centuries, there are the farmers and ranchers of this country providing the bread basket to feed the hungry and starving world, the hardworking men and women of our nation, the brave military and veterans, and the faithful leadership in both business and government, They helped make this country great for you, the next generation, and the generations yet to come.

8

From March to June 2015, there were seventeen GOP presidential candidates that entered their names into the horse race wanting become the Forty-Fifth American President. These are the following GOP candidates: Florida governor Jeb Bush, Dr. Ben Carson famous medical doctor, New Jersey governor Chris Christie, Texas senator Ted Cruz, business lady Carly Florina, Virginia governor Jim Gilmore, South Carolina senator Lindsay Graham, Arkansas governor Mike Huckabee, Louisiana governor Bobby Jindal, Ohio governor John Kasich, Kentucky senator Rand Paul, New York governor George Pataki, Texas governor Rick Perry, Florida senator Marco, Rubio, Pennsylvania senator Rick Santorum, rich businessman Donald Trump, and Wisconsin governor Scott Walker.

Starting with August 2015, these GOP candidates had their national TV debates in the big horse race hopeful to become the Forty-Fifth President of the United States. Now they are getting ready of taken their horses to the starting gate, just waiting for the firing of the gun to start the race to the White House. At first this will be the warm up race of the coming GOP debates during 2015, the big race will be the various state's caucuses and primaries of 2016 and going on to the Cleveland, Ohio July convention then racing on for the Big Election of November 2016.

Now the GOP presidential horse race to the White House is really getting crowded with seventeen candidates at the starting gate. Since there are so many people in this GOP horse race, it might be more excitement and fun just take your grandchildren to the county or state fairs for them ride the merry-go-around. For us "Golden Age" people, we can just be watching the three horse races for the Triple Crown winner on national TV.

There are several GOP underdogs in this crazy wild race to the White House. However, don't count them out of the race, just look back past years ago when Jimmy Carter and Ronald Reagan were running for the presidency. Both of them were underdogs, but they still became presidents of our country.

There were five GOP debates in 2015 on national TV that was held in various cities across our country. The main debates were the top candidates at that time by national polls. The top three or five candidates keep changing positions from one debate to another one as they were discussing the main issues facing America, what they can do for our America and what they can do for you and your family. The GOP start their presidential horse race in the Summer 2015 with seventeen candidates, by March 2016 it was down only to three candidates. These were front runner Donald Trump, second place was Texas senator Ted Cruz, and next was Ohio governor John Kasich. The other fourteen candidates dropped out of the horse race to the White House by stating "This was not their time" and that lack of financial support. Those GOP debates were like the March Madness in college basketball games with the Road to the Final Four, it was the same kind of madness as they went into the many March Super Tuesday elections. One month later, it was down to businessman Donald Trump still in the race to the White House as senator Ted Cruz and governor John Kasich dropped out.

The taxpayers and voters want less fighting among the candidates in any debate and more what America need to hear and what us Americans want from these candidates. All hard working Americans need and want job security with good benefits, stronger American economy, good health care for our family, protection from ISIS terrorism, and a stronger military. If any Democratic or Republican candidate can't do something better for our country, they need to pack their bags and go back home.

There came some bad news for the GOP, John Boehner the Speaker of the House made announcement of his retirement from that position. The GOP asked Rep. Paul Ryan, who was the chairman of the Ways and Means Committee and the 2012 vice president nominee if he want be the next speaker. As a good GOP American, Paul Ryan was elected as the Fifty-Fourth Speaker of the House. He stated that "The Americans made this country work, and the house should work for them."

Just before the July 2016 Cleveland National Convention, businessman Donald Trump had picked Indiana governor Mike Pence as his running mate for vice president. This is a very good choice for this combination working team going into the big November 2016 national presidential race. They had good slogans that of "Making America Great Again" and that of "Making America One Again." Trump added with the following words, "I will fight for you, and I will win for you."

May our GOD Bless America again under the new leadership of the new American President and members of Congress. Always, be sure that you vote for the most faithful person in your local, state, and federal government elections this November 2016 or any future elections.

Since this might be a crazy and unknown election year, just remember in the 2000 election year, Al Gore had more popular votes of 540,000 over George W. Bush, but George Bush ended in the White House as America's President because he accumulated more Electoral College votes. Could this happen again and it might. Our Founding

Fathers set up the Electoral College system to indirectly choose the president. They did not want popular votes or the House of Congress choose the president for our country.

The good news for Hillary Clinton is that a great deal of women would vote for her as the 2016 US president. According to various Gallup polls, people would vote for a lady president. In the year 1968 Gallup poll that 57 per cent would vote for a well qualified woman. That percentage number has been increasing over the years:

- Year 1983—that 80 percent would vote for a qualified woman.
- Year 2007—that 88 percent would vote for a qualified woman.
- Year 2013—that 95 percent would vote for a qualified woman.

June 2015, there were five candidates that entered the Democratic presidential race hopeful becoming the Forty-Fifth President of the United States. These candidates were front runner Secretary of State Hillary Clinton, Rhode Island governor Lincoln Chafee, Maryland governor Martin O'Malley, Vermont senator Bernie Sanders, and Virginia senator Jim Webb. October 2015, Vice President Joe Biden announced he won't run for president. He stated "I will not be silent, we will stand as a party and where we needed to go as a nation."

There were three Democratic main national TV debates during 2015 in various cities across our country. The five candidates were discussing the top topics that was facing our country and what they will do improved our America and make it financial better and safer for your family. Some of these top topics consisting the following: improve America's economy, tax breaks for business and families, gun control, improve borders, and that of ISIS terrorist. By the end of December 2015, the final results of these debates there were only two candidates left hoping become the next American President. They were front runner Secretary of State Hillary Clinton and Vermont senator Bernie Sanders.

Before the July 2016 Brotherly Love City Democratic National Convention (DNC), presidential candidate Hillary Clinton had selected Virginia senator and the former governor of that state Tim Kaine as her running mate for Vice President. He will be a big plus in this campaign, also he can speak Spanish very well.

There will be a big mud-throwing contest in this 2016 election, one of these issues will be that of Benghazi when Hillary Clinton was Secretary of State. After that time, she made a statement "It don't matter," but it does matter from this terrorist attack because four Americans were killed. My question to you, if one of those four were your father, husband, son or brother; how would you feel? This took place just a few weeks before the 2012 National Election, during which the Forty-Fourth President was reelected. Another issue facing Hillary Clinton is that of using e-mail account as Secretary of State which created confusion over when and whether she complied with federal regulation of not forwarding such e-mails to the State Department. This matter is still being review by the FBI as being unlawful act. There may be questions of large money contribution into the Clinton Foundation of where it came from. It maybe that old game on Capitol Hill of wheel and deal, or under the table deals. That is, if you do something for me as give me some of your money and your vote; and I will do something special for you. Also, there are many people who are saying "We don't want another Obama third term and we don't trust her." These maybe some reasons why many people will not vote for her as the next president.

In the twenty-first century, it seems that to become president of our country, it takes the following: what you know, who you know, and lots of Big Money. The Secretary of State has lots of Big Money to back her all the way to the November 2016 election. Another big plus for her is that having lots of advice from her husband the former president Bill Clinton. America's President Bill Clinton had eight years of experience in both on Capitol Hill and that of foreign affairs, he will back her all the way to the July Philadelphia convention and on into the White House as the next American President.

> Fear God and keep His commandments. For this
> the whole duty of man. (Eccles. 12:13)

Going into the final months of this 2016 national presidential election between Secretary of State Hillary Clinton and that of wealthy businessman Donald Trump, it will be like most elections in the past years, many voters can and will change their minds and vote for the other person or just don't vote at all. Changing voter's minds can be based upon the changing issues at that time such as: economic conditions, health care changes, ISIS terrorists, higher coming taxes.

My American citizens, as you vote next November 2016, first pray for a strong Christian business-minded person to become our next president. We must vote for those who are best support of biblical and godly principles. It is a must that Christians should be going to the polls and vote. Let's do it in record numbers. Yes, your vote does count, for this is your America. Do this for your country, your children, and their children. Our America needs a president and members of Congress that will take our nation forward both financial and being military strong again. Always keep our local, state, and federal leaders in your prayers. May God bless America again.

Since I have completed this part of my book, what will take place in the 2016 election and for the next four or eight years under the leadership of the new American President and members of Congress will be written by many other authors. May God Bless the right person to become the new Forty-Fifth President and that person will have the backbone, faith, and wisdom of making our country greater.

Our country is in trouble in this new 21st century more so then in our life time. There seems to be very few leaders who will take a stand for God.

> When the foundations are being destroyed, what can the righteous do? (Ps. 11:3)

Yes, we are seeing issues of what is causing the very foundation to crumple. Yes, its praying time again for our America for we need a good ole fashion revival fire across our land, lets rekindle those revival fires in Jesus name that our county become greater. As you vote in the November 2016 election or any election in the future, just remember those famous words by President John F. Kennedy that of "Ask not what your country can do for you, ask what you can do for your country." Also, those famous words by Dr. Martin Luther King Jr. that of "I have a dream." Let us keep those words alive for America going forward. Most important of all you and your family go from your house to the church house each Sunday and pray for the following words taken from the Bible.

> If my people, who are called by my name, will humble themselves and pray and seek my face and turn from their wicked ways, then I will hear from

> heaven and forgive their sin and heal their land.
> (2 Chron. 7:14)

My dear brothers and sisters in Christ, you are His people, just get on your knees and humble yourself as you are looking toward His face in heaven; that God will Bless America again. For this to take place, you must bless Him first. Just remember, my Christian friends and neighbors always stand up for your Christian believes and pray daily for our America and its leaders.

After more than sixteen years of this new twenty-first century, we have seen so many bad things happen in our country such as the following stock market crashes of years 2000 and 2008, the terrorist attack of 9/11, two wars in Iraq and Afghanistan, the Forty-Fourth President many unknowns of "Change for America," the Great Recession, and the upcoming 2016 election. Our America needs a good morale booster more than ever, and we got one. It was the many messages of faith, hope, love, and for world peace by one person—it was a Man of God, that of Pope Francis. After a four-day visit in Cuba, there were good news coming to America that Pope Francis is coming for a six-day visit to our country. The people's pope, as he is known, will bring faith, hope, and love. He went to Washington, DC, for two days, had mass at St. Matthew, and went next at the joint meeting of Congress on Capitol Hill. He stated that Congress need to help USA grow. His good advice was that citizens build better lives that of the *Golden Rule*. The second trip was to NYC with prayer meeting at St. Patrick's Cathedral, a meeting at United Nations, and a visit at *ground zero*. There he was stating, "It's impossible to live in world peace." In the pope's last two-day trip, he went to Philadelphia of bring "life-changing blessing" message of brotherly love at historic Independence Hall. He held mass at Cathedral Basilica of Saint Peter-Paul. He stated that "families stay together with miracle love." Yes, Pope Francis is the people's pope as he brought faith, hope, and love to all Americans. The Pope requests before going home that we pray for him.

The second part of this book is regarding the time up to the Rapture of His church. I am seeing a big change in the last sixteen years of this twenty-first century for our America during these troubled times. We are living in the end-times, or the last days of this church age. God's big clock in heaven is ticking away; those end-times, or last days, are more here in the early years of this twenty-first century than ever before. That time might be closer to the high noon hour here in America, or someplace else in this world; that time might be closer to the midnight hour. My dear Americans, always be ready and watch out, for the time is near of God's church being caught up in the Rapture. Yes, we all will be gathered together as believers in new bodies just like that of Lord Jesus's. Always, keep looking up, for our Christ is coming soon on that big white cloud in the big sky, to take His church home. Yes, we are almost home.

"Yes, I am coming soon." Amen. Come, Lord Jesus. The grace of the Lord Jesus be with God's people. Amen. (Rev. 22:20–21)

9

Let's continue with this journey of America, this time it is of the future. My dear brothers and sisters in Christ, this journey will take all of us believers into the Rapture of His church. Our Lord Jesus will be coming on a cloud to take us home to heaven, so be watching and always be ready. This will be a journey of a lifetime.

Prophecy is God's way of giving us a fair warning so we can prepare our hearts and minds to be ready for what is ahead. What will be the signs for the end-times and last days of the church age and of Christ Coming?

The disciples were asking Jesus regarding the end-times signs, and his answer was as follows:

> No one knows about that day or hour not even the angels in heaven, nor the Son, but only the Father. As it was in the days of Noah, so it will at the coming of the Son of Man. For in the days before the flood,

people were eating and drinking, marrying and giving in marriage, up to the day Noah entered the ark, and knew nothing about what would happen until the flood came, and took them all away. That is how it will be at the coming of the Son of Man. "Two men will be in the field; one will be taken and the other left. Two women will be grinding with a hand mill; one will be taken and the other left." Therefore keep watch, because you do not on what day your Lord will come. (Matt. 24:36–42)

Watch out that you are not deceived. For many will come in my name, claiming. I am the Christ, and will deceive many. (Matt. 24:4–7)

Watch out that that no one deceived you. Many come in my name, claiming I am he, and will deceive many. When you hear of wars and rumors of wars, do not be alarmed. Such things must happen; but the end is still to come. Nations will rise against nation, and kingdom against kingdom. There will be earthquakes in various places, and famines. These are the beginning of birth pains. (Mark 13:5–8, Luke 21:8–11)

Jesus Christ warned that the number one problem on earth in the last days would be deception. We are seeing these all the time—during the twentieth century and more so in the new twenty-first century. The following are just few of them:

The 1990s were booming years for America's economy. People on Main Street and the investors on Wall Street were seeing good and happy times. The Dow Jones Industrial Average, the S&P 500, and the NASDAQ were breaking all-time highs. By the early spring 2000, the good times came to an end on Wall Street. The final result was a big market crash. It took the stock market of the Dow Jones Industrial Average and the S&P 500 over seven years just to get back and break even from the big bad bear market. As of late April 2015, the NASDAQ stocks after fifteen years was hitting new highs. That was a very long time of just breaking even in the stock market. Wall Street brokers were deceiving investors by pushing those "no sense stocks" to bigger highs when those dot.com companies could never succeeded in the business world and never make a profit. Who on Wall Street were so greedy and guilty of deceiving the average investors of our America? No one on Wall Street went to prison. Maybe the investors were taking a chance with their investments.

It happened again with "Take heed that no one deceives you." It was the big housing boom of 2008. People across America were buying their dream homes with little or no down payments. The big banks and various mortgage companies were saying, "Sign on the bottom line. Don't worry, your dream home will always be increasing in value." When the lower temporary interest rates expired, the homeowners were faced with higher home interest rates.

This led to higher house payments and the homeowners not being able to make their bigger house payments. The next two years, bankruptcy and home forecloses were in the hundred thousands per month, with no end of hitting the bottom in the future. It looks like a game of building your dream home by using a deck of cards, putting cards on top each other of building this house of cards. Just one more card on top, and the house of cards will come crashing down. The Forty-Fourth President and his administration's programs were falling short of reaching their initial target of stopping at 3 to 4 million foreclosures. That created more, bigger write-offs in the billon dollars by the big banks. The federal government bailed out those bigger banks over the years, and the bad news is that nobody from the federal government bailed out the homeowners and the stock market investors.

It was the big banks, the federal government, Fannie Mae, and Freddie Mac that deceived or misled the homeowners across America. This developed into the Great Recession, the worst in the past seventy years for our country and the world. Also, the inability of credit agencies such as Moody's and Standard & Poor's performed their jobs of rating mortgage-backed securities. Those financial organizations should work better and be more honest with the homeowners for the purpose of lowering their home interest rates, which would create lower home payments so families could stay in their homes. These financial organizations were stuck with unwanted homes in the millions. Financial organizations went through the same situation back in the late 1980s and into the early 1990s with the savings and loan firms. Will our banking system and the federal government with Fannie Mae and Freddie Mac ever learn from their mistakes?

Some financial money managers were deceiving or taking advantage of people's lifetime savings by promising bigger monthly and yearly returns on their investments. When it sounds too good, that is the reason to back off and run away fast. In other words, those dreams and hopes will become your nightmares. Always be sure you get reference or check with the Better Business Bureau. There are many good, honest Christian money managers out there that will take care of your golden years for retirement. This is your money, my Americans, that you paid in for your golden retirement years. My favorite money managers is Premier Asset Management of Brentwood, Tennessee. They are an honest and strong Christian team that will take care of your future dreams. For good financial advice, there are people like Dave Ramsey who have written several financial books and write an article in your newspaper each week. Also, Mr. Ramsey does financial seminars. There is also Suze Orman on CNBC each Saturday night with her good financial advice.

You don't believe it can happen to you. Bernard Madoff cheated investors out of $17 billion of their principals, not counting loss of dividends and interest. He took money from investors and then used their money to pay out profits to earlier investors. As long as new money came into the system, it would keep on working. It's based upon the ole Ponzi scheme. Over the years of the twentieth century, there have been many crooked money managers using the Ponzi scheme. They get richer while you get poorer, till they get caught.

Likewise, our own federal government has taken money away from the Social Security fund for other spending programs, paying back with worthless IOUs. Congress has borrowed or stolen an estimated $2.5 trillion from the Social Security Trust Fund, or a total of $5.1 trillion from both Medicare and Social Security funds. Unless we act now, Medicare and Social Security will not be able to promise benefits to seniors in just a few more years. This Ponzi scheme has been around for years, so watch your golden years retirement money and that of your Social Security.

Report on Fox News of February 2015: House Minority Leader Nancy Pelosi made a statement that some members of the US Congress are living payday to payday. Their salary is $174,000 yearly; this is compared to the average family annual income of $55,400. If these Congress people can't manage their own family money, no wonder the US Congress on Capitol Hill can't manage our America's budget.

During all those national political campaigns, people were giving you those hot-air pipe dreams, they are going to do this and that for you and for our America. Recalling a few national elections ago, one person was saying, "I have a plan," but that doesn't explain those plans. The next national election came, and this man was saying "Change for America." Yes, but he did not tell the American voters what those changes will be for America and you and your families. The voters were ready and wanting to make changes. They were mostly the African Americans, Mexicans, the Encore Organization, college-age people, and other young people. He was elected the Forty-Fourth American president. Eight years and still counting, those Changes for America were heartbreakers and disappointing promises for our Americans. The famous humorist Will Rogers once said, "The short memories of American voters is what keeps our politicians in office."

The new plan by this president is taking our country toward socialism: share your wealth with others who have less. It would be the end of capitalism and the end of middle class people. It look like we are living on the edge of tomorrow. It was another of those end time or last days of "take heed that no one deceive you." Now is the time for all Americans start saying "No More" and "Enough is Enough" to our own big fat federal government, for we want a better government not a bigger one.

With the 2016 national election coming up, most Americans want to hear on national TV the debates of how and when you politicians will get our country up and running as a greater and stronger America. All Americans want better-secured jobs with good health and retirement benefit plans, plus homeland security. No more of this deceiving America with false promises. We want more of the honest truth for once.

The nation's corporate tax of 35% is the largest in the world. Corporate America can't afford higher taxes to be competitive in this world economic market. Our American tax code system has almost 75,000 pages—that is big-time insane. Let's put an end of this "no nonsense" tax system. Maybe someday, the Washington DC politicians will come up with a fair and simple federal flat tax that would lower taxes for you and help your family. Every April, Americans go through the misery and the nerve-wracking filing of their yearly income taxes. Just make it simple—a one-page form for the family and two pages for small business owners. America can't trust the IRS anymore. Now is the time to downsize this federal organization. Is this one of those "Be aware of people deceiving you?"

After years of reckless spending, America's debt level is nearing a breaking point, and our nation can't rely on foreign capital as a last resort. Our nation owes China, India, Japan, and the United Kingdom over $5 trillion, plus annual interest. It's bad, my America. We have to borrow about 45 cents for each dollar that our federal government is spending. There's so much bad and wasteful spending by our own government. This *must* stop *now*. My America, there is no rich sugar daddy out there for our country's financial rescue. The people of our America have looked away from our God in heaven and made the federal government their God. Don't count on your Uncle Sam to bail you out again or give you a helping hand. Our Uncle Sam has a bad back of carrying all the financial burdens of our country. My Americans, your great country, the USA, is bankrupt; and the big federal government in Washington DC is broken down in leadership.

In the future years, the federal government will be making adjustments to reduce various services' programs or have higher taxes. These will be programs like Medicare, Medicaid, and Social Security, for they have become very expensive. The poor and the middle class will be the ones that will be hit the hardest and brought to a lower standard of living. Most important of all, my Americans, just keep up with your faith in God. Our good God will take care of his believing children, just only believe that our God is the answer. The bad news is that there will be protests and riots in the streets across America over any government cutbacks. When God is in control, your life is in control. As believers, we need to put any or such problems in God's hands. When our America gives up as a believing country, you will be seeing our America blowing in the wind.

The buck doesn't stop with the president of the United States. The buck stops with the taxpayers and the voters of America—that is us. The government works for you. You are the real boss for firing and hiring. The president, with his administration and members of Congress doesn't understand that job situation of who is the real boss. Just remind them at the next election with your votes. We all must stand firm and tall just like the Bible-believing Founding Fathers of 1776. Our country needs more action and less talk from the president, his staff, and both parties of Congress.

We serve a God who will step out onto the bow of our vessel and say, "Peace. Be still." He is the one that controls the storms of our daily lives, that may be blowing in today and tomorrow. God is that bridge over those troubled waters of our daily lives. Let's put a stop to the federal government raising the floodgates of creating more troubled waters for our America. If the people of our land don't change their sinful ways and the same with the leaders of our big federal government, God will make a bigger change for our country, and it will not be for the best.

My Americans of our great America, we need faithful leadership in our local, state, and federal governments. Such a faithful person who will stand up for what he and she believes in for getting our nation's economy or any other problem back on the recovery road. God will bless such believing people. Just only believe, and God will answer our prayers for the financially uncertain times in our country.

Always keep in mind of those famous words: "Ask not what your country can do for you, ask what you can do for your country." And the words " I have a dream." Let's keep those words alive and have our America going forward, greater and stronger as a World Power country.

People of America, it's in your hands. Let's pray for a faithful America. Lord Jesus, we come to you in your name for a believing, better, and greater America. Our country needs a spirit filled and an uplifting revival for our America. We are lacking a faithful, business-minded leadership from the courthouse, the schoolhouse, the house of Congress, and the White House. We must get on our knees in our church houses every Sunday across this country and be praying for our America and our leaders in Washington DC. Lord Jesus, with our crying eyes, wipe away those tears as we are praying that you have mercy for our country by answering our daily prayers for a faithful and greater America. Thank You, Lord Jesus.

We want a church and a nation that has victory in Jesus. Lord, we will get on our knees in prayer, for we still want those words "In God We Trust" for our country. Yes, there is still hope for our country. My Americans, let's keep those dreams, hopes, and visions alive. Our Lord Jesus will provide with more blessings and healings in our lives and for our America.

10

THE FEDERAL GOVERNMENT needs to be doing a better job of providing good jobs with good benefits for Americans here in our homeland, improving our education system for students who will have a brighter future, and with reasonable cost for medical care with good-paying doctors and nurses. We don't want any more of those unfulfilled promises of deceiving people at election time or anytime. This is no time for kicking the can down the road, for what we want is the truth, the whole truth.

The well-paying white-collar jobs are disappearing at an alarming rate. The main causes of this trend is changing automation and technology; also by sending well-paying jobs to low-cost centers abroad. It's global competition from emerging economics from Brazil, China, and India that will force Americans to change their standard of living. The good news is that over the years, we are seeing technology improvements. The factory workers today are more productive than their fathers during their time on the assembly line. Let's give those small businesses and corporations a good tax credits as they are making productive improvements on the assembly factory floor, and tax breaks for keeping jobs here in our homeland of America. Now is the time to change our corporate federal tax of 35 percent to a lower rate. Our America would be more competitive with the rest of the world, and this would enable corporations to increase productions and hire more people. The working consumer would be buying more goods and services for their families. Yes, Uncle Sam will get his share in taxes.

John Rockefeller Jr. said, "I believe in the dignity of labor, whether with head or hand, that the world owes no man a living but it owes every man an opportunity to make a living."

America needs keep improving its education system at the high school, vocation school, and junior college levels by providing skills job training to keep jobs here on the home front. We are seeing an increase in homeschooling of kids. The estimate number for homeschooling in the year 2015 is over 2 million kids, and growing at a rate of 8 percent per year. Study shows that these kids are better employees with strong work ethics. There is talk in Washington DC that the president wants free two-year community college, which will be a big plus for students seeking their carriers. Cost for higher education has for years been increasing faster than the average national rate of inflation, and that cost keeps going up each year. The colleges and universities across our land must work better in controlling the cost for higher education. When it takes more than four years or about five years get a BS degree from any college or university, it's due to poor management at the college level. It's time to reorganize the number of credit hours and offer the necessary courses at the right time for students to graduate in less than four years. With my GI Bill, I received a degree in accounting from Ball State University by going school year around and finishing up in three years. That was in the year 1960. What has changed in the fifty-five-plus years?

It's also true with cost of medical care, each year higher than the year before and increasing faster than the national average of inflation. The day is coming in the near future when our big federal government will be cutting back on programs such as Medicare and Medicaid. The Forty-Fourth President said that he will not pull the medical plug on Grandma, but the government will be cutting medical care programs, which will become the slow death for the elderly and poor people of America. We don't want to hear any more talk on Capitol Hill in Washington DC of cutting back on the medical care programs because of our huge uncontrollable national debt. My family doctor is telling me that he has half the patients compared to prior years because of government paperwork and unnecessary red tape regulations. Many doctors are quitting their medical practices and working for the local hospitals. This has happened to my medical doctor. The latest report as of March 2015 from NBC is that one-third of the doctors in America will be retiring by year 2025. Also, less men and women are going into the medical field , because they will be in debt of $200,000 after finishing medical school. This will be a big concern for all Americans in the near future—a big shortage of both doctors and nurses. Several hospitals across our country have had to lay off employees in the last few years because of payment cuts of ObamaCare. We will be seeing more expensive medical care, and people will be waiting longer for medical care in doctor's offices and hospitals.

The Forty-Fourth President's administration requiring health insurance coverage for contraceptions, which is being challenged in court by several religious groups. One of these is the Little Sisters of the Poor regarding religious freedom. Who will win this court case, the Big Brothers in Washington DC or the Little Sisters of the Poor? Yes, Little Sisters, we will be praying for you and that the good God bless you.

During the Great Recession years, not one word from the president, his administration, and members of Congress that they were willing to take a cut in their salary or their rich medical care program and pension plans. When it comes to cutting back on spending, who comes first, the big federal government or you? Yes, it's always you.

The biggest priority for our America is creating more and better jobs, but our Forty-Fourth President and his administration during his first year of office start deceiving America with his Obamacare. They had done this behind locked doors in secret meetings, by creating several thousands of pages of medical "Do this and don't do that" for your future medical care. At the same time, making no changes to their own rich medical plans. According to corporate America and small business, they can't afford this new medical plan for their working employees and retirees. This means that small businesses and corporations will be cutting back on their medical insurance programs for active and retired employees and their families. What will happen to America's future medical plans such as Medicare and Medicaid is very uncertain. My dear Americans, expect more changes such as higher premiums, deductibles, and an increased in copayments from insurance companies. Changes for Medicare are on the way. Starting in 2018, people with annual income over $133,500 will be paying higher premiums for both doctors' visits and prescriptions. Few years ago, our Forty-Fourth President made the promise that "your family would be saving $2,500 a year on medical care." That is one crazy promise to make. What do you call that, deception or one big lie?

The biggest insured, United Health Group, may quit Obamacare after the year 2016. This exit could affect over or some 540,000 people, who are heavy users of this medical care program. The big question is, Which will be the next insured company that will have cuts in medical care or dropping out Obamacare plan? All this means that more money will be coming out of your pockets for medical care for yourself, your family, or paying for other people medical insurance through higher taxes.

Since the Forty-Fourth President's reelection in the 2012 national election, there has been very little chance of revising this no-sense medical plan. Many states of America are suing the federal government on this ObamaCare medical insurance program. It's a program where if you don't buy medical insurance from the federal government, they will fine you or tax you to death. This fine or tax will be increasing each year if you don't buy or have health insurance. Mr. President, you can't buy medical insurance without a job. The problem with ObamaCare is that it requires employers with more than fifty full-time employees to provide their employees/families with health insurance. That requirement is that a full-time employee is one working thirty-hour weeks, not the established standard forty-hour week. The problem with this health program is that it will make small businesses have their employees work less than thirty hours per week in order for the business owners not to pay this health insurance. It could happen, and it will.

Again, under the Affordable Care Act, there is Health Insurance Tax (TIP), which is a direct tax on small business. This tax will cost small business 500 dollars per employee per year. This will be a big burden on small businesses, where health insurance is already on the increase each year. Here in Tennessee, there are about 566,000 small businesses that will be hit hard with TIP. My America, we need faithful, good, honest businessmen and businesswomen to be our leaders in our local, state, and federal governments. If not, we will see our America blowing in the wind.

My America, we need to get on our knees and pray for our country. We are living in troubled times. Our God is the only real answer to our country's economic conditions for He is the bridge over those troubled waters. We don't know what tomorrow holds, but God has all the tomorrows in his big, caring hands. Our God is in control, and He knows the future. Just put your faith in His hands. My dear Americans, just feed your faith and starve your doubts. Let's build a better America for your children and their children. This is no time be sitting on our hands or going back to bed, because our America is on its deathbed. We have a bankrupt nation with a broken-down and confused federal government.

> "No eye has seen, no ear has heard, no mind has conceived what God has prepared for those who love him." But God has revealed it to us by his Spirit (1 Cor. 2:9–10).

This is the confidence we have in approaching God: that if we ask for anything according to his will, he hears us. And if we know that he hears us, whatever we ask, we know that we have what we asked of him (1 John 5:14–15)

11

It's a shame that our country has to borrow money from foreign countries and print more dollars in order that our big federal government can spend or waste more money. We are borrowing 45 cents for every dollar we spend. There was a budget surplus during the rich time of the 1990s under the Bill Clinton presidency, but two recessions, small tax cuts, 9/11 of two wars, and the government's expensive stimulus program brought the budget into red ink. There will not be a surplus budget again in our country. The national debt going into the year 2016 is $19 trillion plus paying interest on that borrowed money. If this is the same path that our country has been going in last few years, our national debt will be over $30 trillion within the next ten years. Our country can't afford these big-time spenders in Washington, DC, by using our hard-earned tax money for crazy, unnecessary spending.

No wonder we are seeing Americans protesting at Town Hall meetings and the Tea Party rallies across the nation. They were saying to the government, "We don't trust you anymore." When you are ready to vote in any November national or state election, pray first, for we need men and women that love God and fear Him. It's time to stop this backstabbing, finger pointing, and blaming each party over this and that. This financial mess started several years ago with bad policy by both parties, but it's time to take responsibility. After years of reckless spending, America's debt level is nearing a breaking point, and our country can no longer rely on foreign countries lending out money as a last resort for our country. It will get to a point sometime in the future when no country will want to lend money to America, unless our USA has to trade their money for our prime land and real estate. We don't want that to happen, for this is our land.

The only way out of any financial trap is for the local, state, and federal governments to balance their own budgets by cutting expenses and reducing business, corporate, and personal taxes. We need to get rid of all this unnecessary red tape and regulations that give our business leaders a big headache. We want a better federal government, not a bigger one, for that is the biggest problem facing America. The final resort is to lower taxes will create better and more jobs for our country. Otherwise, many Americans will have to learn to live on less and take a hit on their standard of living.

Since the federal government is having a hard time to balancing its yearly budgets on time, there is a new plan on Capitol Hill that by the year 2017 Congress wants to revise the budget system from a one-year to a two-year plan. They have not okayed a budget and funding bill on time since 1997.

The Forty-Fourth President and his administration has progressively taken over education, energy, and health care. It is time for Americans to rise up and say "No more" or "Enough is a enough" and "Let's turn this country around." America is still the greatest country in the world, and we need representatives who stand on their own two feet and not be sitting on their two hands. It's high time, Mr. President. You need to be doing a better job on your homework before going public talking about America's economy or any other subject. Just tell it as it really is. We, the people of America, want hear the real whole truth for once. Each time you and members of Congress open your mouth to talk, it seems you are always putting your foot in it or shooting yourselves in the foot.

Remember, "Take heed that no one deceives you." We are seeing this more than ever.

Our federal government needs to be smarter and wiser. When the Forty-Fourth President and his administration approved the half-billion-dollar business loan to Solyndra, a few months later, this corporation filed for bankruptcy and laid off all 1,100 of its employees. Good business practice by the banks or the government is to always check the business balance sheet and profit-loss statement before making loans. Several additional solar companies were getting similar loans from our big crazy federal government. This administration was providing lots of handouts without doing any homework. It's our hard-earned tax money that is being wasted; it is not the government's money to be spent or wasted.

The final result from all this big national financial mess, our great America is bankrupt. Our federal government is spending more money than they bring in from taxes and selling U.S. Treasury bonds and notes. The difference for the make up is borrowing from other countries such as China, India, and Japan. Some day that oversea borrowing will come to a big sudden halt. They will never trust our government again, because we can't afford to pay borrow money back or even pay the higher interest rates on those loans. Our federal government has run out of silver bullets of fixing the economy or any problems. They need take lesson from the Lone Ranger for he never run out of silver bullets.

Sometime down the road, all Americans, both the old and the young will be facing a lower standard of living. During this twenty-first century, our country went through two big, bad bear stock markets and two recessions, and it took a big financial toll on baby boomers' and retirees' savings. The big government will be forced to cut back or make major changes in the following programs: food stamps, Medicare, Medicaid, Social Security, and unemployment benefits. Also, the federal government will be revising the tax code of reducing or taking away tax credits for charity, child care, medical deductions, mortgage interest deductions, and other various tax credits. What all this means is a big tax increase is coming for America. Such government cutbacks will create greater hardship for the poor and middle-class people of America. That old game of hide-and-go-seek that kids used to play, someone would say, "Ready or not, here I come." Yes, this time it will not be the kids. It will be the big federal government saying, "Ready or not, here we come."

Please take time to read your Bible each day with your family, God has an answer for the dark storms in your life. The end-times or last days of this church age is *now*, for it's happened in your lifetime of this twenty-first century. If you and your family have financial, medical, and personal needs, just pray about those needs for our God will provide. Our God is in control and he knows all the tomorrows, he will take care of you today and for ever. We need good old-fashioned fire-up revival in our country to bring it back to what our God wants for us. With greater faith, God will bless your family and give freedom and living peace for our America. We must put our faith and trust in God's hands, the good Lord will provide for our needs.

A few months of the fall season 2011, the Forty-Fourth President selected twelve members of Congress, known as the Super Committee, to work out a sound working economic program for getting our nation going forward being financially and militarily stronger. The deadline was Thanksgiving Day, a couple of days before that big due day the Super Committee throw up their hands and gave up. The Super Twelve Committee became known as the Dirty Dozen. January 2012 because our nation economy was growing very slowly, the Federal Reserve stated that a full economic recovery could take at least three more years. It seems that our big federal government just can't do anything right. My question to my dear Americans is this: "Do you not trust your federal government anymore, and are you tired of those deceiving promises of what they can do for your country and for you?" If so just voted them out of the office at the next national election; please stand up and let your opinions for our America be heard and seen.

For over two hundred years, the American Indians have a good saying: "The great white father in Washington speaks with forked tongue." The white men killed off their buffalo, and the people in Washington put them in "No-man's-land reservations." They were the most mistreated of all Americans in our land. After many broken promises for the American Indians, how true is that saying. The bad news is that it is still true today for all Americans as we keep hearing words to our federal government, "We don't trust you anymore," and for those politicians in Washington DC who still "speak with forked tongue."

The only answer for turning our America around is to put those economic conditions or any other problems in the hands of our Lord Jesus. America must hear the truth more than ever, the truth will set our country free. Say, you politicians on Capitol Hill of Washington DC, do you know the truth? Maybe that is why you can't sleep at night?

The summer of 2015, the US Supreme Court made the decision of the same-sex marriage rights with a vote of 5 to 4 to be applied for all fifty states. Polls show that a majority of Americans want to see the higher court of our land to make a final ruling. It will vote over whether states can continue defining marriage as the union of one man and a woman, or give gay and lesbian couples the right to marry. Prior to this decision by the higher court that same-sex couples could marry in thirty-six states and the District of Columbia, many church pastors, ministers, and priests don't like doing/having same-sex marriage. They like those couples, but don't like the sin. The higher court was forced to vote what the Forty-Fourth President wanted, not what is right according to God? Many county clerks across the nation are quitting their jobs for they don't want to marry same-sex couples.

According to God, marriage is between one man and one woman. Children need both a father and a mother so they can have better education, emotional stability, and good Christian morals. Doing things together as one big happy family makes a better country.

> "So God created man in his own image, in the image of God he created him; male and female he created them. God blessed them and said to them, 'Be fruitful and increase in number." (Gen. 1:27–28)
>
> For this reason a man will leave his father and mother and be united to his wife, and they will become one flesh. (Gen. 2:24)

Churches could face penalties, or even lose their tax exempt status, for failing to conduct same-sex weddings. The same with small business such as bakers, photographers, and restaurants for not allowing such wedding services.

What took place in our country back in the 1960s, the 1970s, and up today with declining Christian morals, that over the decades later we were reaping what we had been sowing. The US Supreme Court took away the Bible and prayer out of schools, approved abortion of killing unborn babies, now they will be forced to approve same-sex marriage. Who is the judge of our land—is it the courts or God? The higher court of the land have forgotten one big issue— how will same-sex couples affect the children who will not have a father and a mother in the same home? According to our Bible regarding to same-sex marriage, God does not approved of it. Homosexual practice is sinful in God's eyes. It looks like our America is being deceived again by the higher court of the land. Let's pray for the wisdom of God to work into the hearts and minds of the US Supreme Court to bring our America back to the ways of God.

> Shameful lusts for women exchanged natural relations for unnatural ones. In the same way the men also abandoned natural relations with women and inflamed with lust for another. Men committed indecent acts with other men, and received in themselves the due penalty for their perversion. (Rom. 1:26–27)

> And this is love: that we walk in obedience to his commands. As you heard from the beginning, his command is that you walk in love. (2 John 1:6)

As a God-believing country, we must keep our dreams, hopes, and vision alive. We want our God, the Bible, prayers, and the Ten Commandments back again across our America in courthouses, schoolhouses, the White House, and the house of Congress. The best place to start is with your house going to the church every Sunday. It's time to stand firm and tall for our rights, that of freedom of the press, freedom of religion, and freedom of speech.

When the foundation are destroyed, what can the righteous do? (Ps. 11:3)

The big Cover-Up Story by the Forty-Fourth President, Secretary of State, the CIA, and most of the TV press (except Fox News) regarding the four American men that were killed by terrorists in Libya on September 11, 2012. This happened prior to the November 2012 national election. As of May 2016, what really happened on that day has not been solved, or it is still a big cover-up story. Again, your America is being deceived big-time. My question to America: "If one of those four American men that were killed in Libya was your brother, father, husband, or son would you voted for the Forty-Fourth President for another four more years?"

It's praying time for our America, that our God will bless and heal our nation. Let's proudly put those great words "In God we trust" back into our nation. Every courthouses across our nation should have those powerful words on display inside and outside their building. We just came off the fiscal cliff, so let's be praying more for our moral and spiritual cliffs that is facing our America. With all the godlessness in our America, there is still hope for our country. Just pray in Jesus's name and have your church be praying each Sunday for our leaders in Washington DC.

The national election of November 2014 is now in the history books. The taxpayers and voters of America came to the polls to vote. They were saying, "No more" and "Enough is enough, we are tired of being deceived year after year." America got the final results: the GOP won big-time and had taken control both of the House and the Senate, plus a few more Republican governors who won in their states. Mr. President, America is not happy with your job, the people came in with a broom and cleaned the House of Congress, and next, the American people will take a broom to clean out the White House come November 2016.

12

ANOTHER OF THOSE end-time signs was this: "you will hear of wars and rumors of wars" (Matt. 24:6, Mark 13:8).

Our country has seen many battles and wars in the last three hundred plus years, for the purpose of this book will start with those two wars of the new 21th century.

This took place on September 11, 2001, with the bombing of the World Trade Center Twin Towers in New York City. That was the day when our country and the rest of the world stood still for a different kind of war—that against terrorism. It was two hijacked planes that flew into the twin towers in New York City, another plane flew into the Pentagon in Washington DC, the passengers of the fourth plane overcame the hijackers, causing the plane to crash in a Pennsylvania field instead of reaching its Washington DC target. This terrorist attacks, caused the deaths of almost 3,000, people including children, and the final resort was to wage two wars against terrorism.

Those terrorists' main game plan was to defeat the enemy that is the USA by destroying the enemy's economy. Their war plan was to take the United States from being the world's largest economy and superpower to a second-tier country in a decade or less.

The Afghanistan War began October 2001, with the United States and the United Kingdom troops combining their military forces to fight for world peace. The main aim of the invasion was to find Osama bin Laden and his high-ranking al-Qaeda members, destroying its organization, and the removal of the Taliban. Our USA military did find bin Laden, and he was killed; but there are many others just as bad, or maybe worse than, their leader. The American president and his administration will have up to ten thousand American troops until 2016 as a supported group in that country.

During the time of that war, or any war, our fighting warriors need the full armor of God as they go out into the battlefield. As you stand your ground against the enemy, be strong in the Lord. Be sure as you are facing the enemy with flaming arrows coming toward you that you have the full armor of God. Always wear your belt of truth, carry your shield of faith, wear your helmet of salvation, and carry the sword of the Spirit. God will be there with you, for God is your Heavenly Commander in Chief. Your family and friends back home will be in prayer for your safe and fast return, and may God Bless you as you serve our country.

The Iraq War was a military campaign authorized by Congress on October 2002. The invasion was led by United States and Great Brittan troops. The main purpose was to search for weapons of mass destruction and overthrow of Iraq's dictator, Saddam Hussein. Almost nine years later, the Forty-Fourth President of the United States declared an end to the Iraq combat operation. What great news after such a long, costly war with the loss of many of our brave military men and a cost of over $1 trillion. As of February 2015, our country still has few thousand troops in Iraq for training purposes to fight the terrorists of the ISIS.

The total cost of those two wars will be about $2 trillion, plus the loss of American military lives and the wounded. The reconstruction cost will be in the billions of dollars. Most of those fighting warriors have been in the war zone more than three to eight times. Our wounded fighting warriors will be facing medical and mental conditions and concerns for many years to come, with little or no medical care from VA hospitals. Lack of medical staff owing to 41,500 job vacancies for doctors, nurses, and other medical professionals providing medical at VA Hospitals, the total death toll of those two wars is over 6,700 and with the wounded over 52,200 fighting warriors as of May 2015.

There have been many battles of war in my lifetime in the past eighty-plus years. For any kind of battle, our military needs to put on the full armor of God for protection and safety. During World War II, our military were in fox holes or charging up the hill with their rifle in hand. The wars of the new twenty-first century is a new kind of warfare—that of terrorism. We still need full armor of God. We still need our God to be there on the battlegrounds with our fighting warriors and given total support to their families and friends back home.

The rumors of wars in this new twenty-first century, between North Korea and South Korea, and between North Korea and the United States. Also, there are the war rumors between Iran and Israel, and Iran with United States and Great Britain. During 2014 and into the year 2015, with the war of Russia against the Ukraine; there seems to be no time for peace. The year 2015, the terrorist attacks by ISIS, beheading or killing Christians by the hundreds, including children, in Iraq and Syria. Taking women as sex slaves, the ISIS has no problem acquiring personnel, money, and weapons. The ISIS is becoming public enemy number one in the world. In September 2015, the world saw on the TV news that ISIS attacked several places in Paris, France, killing 129 and wounded 350 people. Again, in March 2016 ISIS terrorists attacked twice in Brussels at a busy airport and at a subway train station. The final results of that killing were 30 (including some Americans) and wounded almost 300 people.

According to a May 2015 by Fox News stated that ISIS are already in America, ready to attack anytime and anywhere. Yes, it did happen in America, the worst attack since 9/11. It was December 2015. ISIS attacked a community service center in San Bernardino, California, with the death of fourteen people and wounded seventeen. Again in June 2015, ISIS-related gunman went into a gay nightclub located in Orlando, Florida. The final results of all that shooting was fifty-three people were dead, leaving forty-nine wounded—some of them in critical condition. It was the worst shooting and killing in our country history. Physicians at Orlando Medical Center describe it as a "war scene." Those medical people done an outstanding job taken care of so many people under those stressful conditions.

ISIS is not going away; this is the biggest change/threat of the twenty-first century that is facing America and rest of the world. In order to win against ISIS, we need to know the enemy better, and we need to know their ways better and always be on guard and be ready of any attack. World peace will only come after the Rapture of His Church. Come, Lord Jesus, Come soon.

Iran might be the greatest threat of future wars over the issue of oil. In the early months of 2012, Iran continued to threaten to close the Strait of Hormuz. This is a production of 17 million barrels of oil per day, or one-fifth of the world's total production. North Africa and the Middle East countries are the home of the largest oil production in the world, they export about quarter of world oil. The time will come in the near future, we will be seeing increasing tension between Iran and Israel causing the cost of oil hitting new highs. If and when gas is above $5 a gallon, our America and the rest of the world will be facing real hardship; and that would put the world economy into a big recession. The Near East wars always seem to be over black gold. Without oil, the world economy would come to an end in just a few days.

In April 2015, the aircraft carrier USS *Theodore Roosevelt* was off the shores of Yemen, with nine warships to prepare to intercept potential shipments of Iranian weapons. If Iranians are delivering any weapons, they are violating United Nations resolutions. This naval action might have some ramifications on the nuclear weapons deal between Iran and the World Power countries including America. Also, this part of the world is rich in oil-producing countries, and it might have some effect on the cost of export of oil. The Forty-Fourth President calls this naval action "Freedom of Sea." If this created some kind of naval battles, there goes that Freedom at Sea.

The US Army has plans to cut 40,000 soldiers from its ranks over the next two years. Our army will have 450,000 by year 2017. The reduction is due to Pentagon budget cuts. As we are reducing the number of our military's fighting heroes, the ISIS is adding to their military in other countries, including here in America. We saw this here in

Chattanooga, Tennessee, this summer 2015. Heavily armed attackers killed four US Marines and one US Navy person, and wounded other people at all branched recruiting center. As all this is taking place, the ISIS now has a training camp for teenage boys, where they teach these boys how to behead people using dolls.

Those war battles of the old days in Israel, to that of our Fighting Warriors in our 21st century. It reminds me of the Bible story of Saul and the Israelites assembled to fight the Philistine army in the Valley of Elah. The Israelites occupied one hill and the Philistines another hill, with the Valley of Elah in between them. The enemy had a champion of a nine foot giant with his full armor to fight against Saul and his army. God had other plans for this battle as He gather a young shepherd boy, name David, to come up against the giant Goliath.

> David said to the Philistine, "You come against me with sword and spear and javelin, but I come against you in the name of the Lord Almighty, the God of the armies of Israel, who you defied. This day the Lord will hand you over to me, and I will srike you down and cut off your head. Today I will give the carcasses of the Philisitine army to the birds of the air and the beasts of the earth, and the whole world will know that there is a God in Israel." As the Philistine moved closer to attack him, David ran quickly toward the battle line to meet him. Reaching into his bag and taken out a stone, he slung it and

> struck the Philistine on the forehead. The stone sank into his forehead, and he fell facedown on the ground. (1 Sam. 17:45–49)

Yes, there is a God anytime, anywhere for both our military and their family back home, for He is always there for us. Our good God was there with our fighting heroes in the foxholes years ago, and He is there in the battlegrounds of the twenty-first-century wars. If He was there for David against Goliath and the Philistine army many years ago, our God will be there for our military today as they fight for our America's freedom and liberty for the future of all Americans. May God bless our military and their families, plus the veterans of all wars.

Since the founding of the US military under General George Washington, chaplains have shared the faith and ministered to the spiritual needs of our military, especially those fighting warriors of all wars. According to a February 2015 report of Freedom Alliance, all that may change. The vital work of the military chaplains my soon be a crime punishable by court marshal, and possible imprisonment! Now we are seeing the Bibles banned at Walter Reed Military Medical Center. Also, the removal of the words "So help me God" from the Air Force Academy oath sworn by new recruits. In time, or it may be happening now, chaplains will be forbidden from discussing spiritual matters involved in leading a military person or their family to Christ or to strengthen their faith.

Our military both men and women are putting their lives in danger as they go into battle. They need to be wearing the full armor of faith and put their trust in God's hands. Since the year 2008, our country and the military has been in need of a really good commander in chief who has strong Christian values, not a little commander in chief who has no use for Christians. The shield of faith is our Bible. Take the time to read your Bible daily for the word of our Living God and His son Jesus Christ. As Christians, we must be praying for our leaders in Washington DC every day.

The last six years of the Forty-Fourth President's term, we had three men serve as secretary of defense. Now, as of December 2014, this president has appointed another secretary of defense. It looks like this Forty-Fourth President is not doing a good job as commander in chief of our military. Maybe those last three men lost their faith and hope for the world policy leadership of the president. How about the faith and hope for our military, their family, and veterans, these are the Fighting Heroes; our country must take good care of them. The new Secretary of Defense, Mr. Ashton Carter, has come up with a proposal for our U.S. military having a 401K pension plan and incentives for cyber warriors. The purpose is to attracting and retaining troops with skills needed to fight modern day warfare. With the new plan which may be few years away, the Pentagon will match 5 per cent of military pay after two years, with full vesting after six years. Plus a mid career and twenty years large cash bonus. Under the present pension plan, most of our enlistees and half of uniformed officers receive no retirement payments with less than twenty years services. Uncle Sam will be saving billions of dollars by trimming the military pension payments. What is good for our Fighting Heroes, should be good for our President, his Administration, and all members of Congress; they all should have the same pension plan.

According to a February 2015 report published in the *Military Times*, it indicated that moral is down among US troops. Within the last five years, our military men are saying they feel underpaid, underequipped, and underappreciated. In April 2015, a survey by *USA Today* indicated that more than half of the estimated number 770,000 soldiers are pessimistic about their future in the military and unhappy about their jobs. After over fourteen years of war, all military volunteers are going through a time of their life with uncertainty. Because of these two wars of terrorism, we are seeing an increase in suicide and mental illness among servicemen. These conditions are very sad. It's time right now for the commander in chief of America to do something about it. Otherwise, he is not doing a good job of taking care of our fighting heroes and their family.

Since 9/11, the federal government has done many things right with homeland security. Just because we have not had another major attack does not mean we are free from future terrorist attacks. Our country has come a long ways since that sad day of September 11, 2001. We must have the best of homeland security for the safety of our citizens here in America. The latest report from Fox TV News as of June 2015 tells us that airport security are not doing a good job in screening people as they getting to fly out to other places. This must change for the better and the safety of our American people and property.

There are real hardships for the military families back home. The wounded soldiers are not getting proper medical care. The military have been discharging troops who have combat stress, but they are not getting the proper treatment. That means many have major health conditions, including posttraumatic stress disorder and traumatic brain injury. They have left the military service without both a good, proper medical diagnoses and the best medical benefits. Many VA hospital across America are not doing a good a job of providing timely medical care. There are several reports that our military heroes have given up without any hope and have taken their own lives.

Many veterans of the two wars of this new twenty-first century who have returned home can't find a good job, mostly due to the downturn in the economy or because companies are afraid to hire them. The unemployment rate for veterans at one time was about 12 percent. This is a sad condition facing these fighting warriors and their families. What is the commander in chief and the Congress doing for the veterans and their family? Never before has an American president ruled instead governed. Maybe the commander in chief needs to be busted down to the rank of buck private.

Another concern for our military family are the loan sharks near their homebases, charging higher interest rates on loans. Many of our fighting warriors are seeing their dream homes in foreclosures. If those brave fighting warriors are good enough to fight for our freedom and liberty, the government should be good enough to take care of them and their families. America, let's honor and always remember our military and the veterans who fought for our freedom and liberty.

The American Legion is an outstanding organization—it's the largest and most respected veterans organization in the country. The American Legion is committed to serving the needs of veterans and their family, promoting patriotism, protecting American values in communities across this great America, and ensuring a strong national security. What a great purpose for our country, I am a member of American Legion Post 46 here in Cookeville, Tennessee. We still want greater freedom and liberty for our country. Otherwise, you will be seeing your America blowing in the wind.

My dear Americans lets get more involved in helping our military and the veterans. I am financial supporting the following: the Disable Americans Veterans, the USO, and now the Wounded Warrior Project. There are 180 USO Centers and locations around the world, serving as a "Home away from home" for our troops and their families. There are over 200,000 military people that are station overseas, they like make phone calls back home to love ones. There are over 50,000 GIs that were wounded in Afghanistan/Iraq are facing numerous surgeries, months in the hospital, rehabilitation, and counseling. These kinds of stories are no longer on the front pages and nightly newscasts, but let's don't forget these fighting warriors. I extend financial help to these military organizations because I am a Korean War veteran, and I am proud to be an American; and it was my duty to serve my country, and it still is my and your duty to help our veterans.

The saddest condition for our America in the last few years, the Westboro Kansas Church protesting across the country against military funerals. It's based upon the right for the freedom of speech, our own US Supreme Court ruled in favor of the protesters that of the First Amendment. To put someone who is grieving in such a position, dishonor the memory of someone who have given his or her life in defense of their country. Shame to the no sense U.S. Supreme Court and the evil-minded people of Westboro Kansas Church. My question to these kinds of unfaithful people: how is God going to judge you?

Where are you going America? This country was founded on the beliefs in Freedom of Religion and "In God we trust," now we are seeing our America Blowing in the Wind. Why, my dear Americans that we can't say "No more" or "Enough is enough" to the very few people that don't have good Christian values? We need to stand firm and tall on the principles of our Founding Fathers, that of the freedom of religion, freedom of the press, and freedom of speech. My dear Americans lets get more involved, now is the time for you be saving our freedom and liberty, for it's your America.

After the Rapture of His Church, there will be the War of all Wars, it will between most of the world coming together against Israel, which is God's holy land. Lord Jesus will come down from heaven with His army of saints for that great War of all Wars. The believers that are born again or saved who was caught up in the Rapture, we will be riding white horses with our Lord Jesus in that great War of all Wars.

Then they gathered the kings together to the place that is called Amageddon. I saw heaven open and there before me was a white horse, whose rider is called Faithful and True. The armies of heaven were to following him, riding on white horses. They go out to the kings of the whole world to gather them for the battle on the great day of God Almighty.

We don't want oil risen to $150 or more per barrel, or gas above 5 dollars per gallon and hold at those level for months, it could set off another world depression. The world economy grows or slows down with the price and supply/demand of black oil. Without this one commodity, there will always be wars and rumors of wars between countries around the world.

Take time each day to pray for the safety of America, our citizens, our troops, and for the return of a godly country. All churches across our country should take few minutes each Sunday morning and evening services to pray for our country and our leaders. Keep praying for world peace as we are seeing chaos in Syria, the ISIS in Iraq, and America, and the greater tension seen in Israel. These are difficult times in this twenty-first century. We are a believing people wanting a country in victory and a winning America. See our crying eyes and hear our prayers, Lord Jesus. Have mercy that you will bless and heal our land, again.

Let's put our hand to the plow and sow faith seeds in rich black soil, plow deep and wide that those faith seeds will have deeper roots, for a greater and stronger America. It take a lot of faith for people to stand up for their beliefs. It's time for all Christians to take the time to get on their knees and look up toward heaven to pray for our America. We want a country of the brave and proud. Let's take pride in our beliefs that we have a greater vision for our America. We must become more believing and faithful so that we can have an America that is united, that is victorious—a winning nation that will go forward.

> "Yet even now," declares the Lord, "return to me with your heart." (Joel 2:12)

13

WHAT ARE THE other signs of end-times? "Earthquakes in various places" (Matt. 24:7, Mark 13:8).

Don't recall any time in my lifetime when there were so many storms in our country. They have been occuring more often and with greater force, causing greater financial damage and much loss of life. Late August 2005 came with bad news for New Orleans, Hurricane Katrina was devastating, and the recovery took a long time. This hurricane killed more than 1,800 people, damaged 500,000 homes along the Gulf Coast with a cost more than $151 billion damages, and leaving 80 percent of New Orleans underwater. Then more bad news came again in September 2005, when Hurricane Rita did extensive damage near the Louisiana-Texas border. Two hurricanes in the summer of 2014 were heading for Hawaii, the first one in the last twenty-two years.

The April 2015 forecasters from Colorado State University have predicted well below average for the Atlantic hurricane season of seven tropical storms. Of which only three will become hurricanes. This is good news, for the average is twelve tropical storms and seven hurricanes per season according to records going back from 1950 to the present.

October 2015 major flooding and historic rainfall up to two feet from the category 2 Hurricane Joaquin that hit South Carolina. This became known as "the 1,000 year storm." At that time, the death toll of ten or maybe more and millions of South Carolinians remained homebound. Also from this major storm, a cargo ship had sunk near the Bahamas in the brutal seas and high winds of Hurricane Joaquin. It is believe that all thirty-three crew members, including twenty-eight Americans aboard came down with the ship. The strongest hurricane ever recorded in the Western Hemisphere that of category 5, Hurricane Patricia hit the Mexico's Pacific Coast in October 2015. Tens of thousands of people were being evacuated. It missed two populated cities and slammed into an inland Mexico mountain range, which weaken the storm. Because of the evacuations and that this major hurricane hit the mountain range, it saved many lives. The remnants of Hurricane Patricia moved on into the states of Texas, Louisiana, Mississippi, Alabama, and the Florida Panhandle, causing major and life-threatening flooding from very heavy rainfall.

The last few years have seen tornadoes in places not seen before, and they did major property damage and loss of lives. As of late spring 2011, there have been almost 1,200 tornadoes across the USA, more than 750 of them in April that year. The average is 150 for April. The year 2011 was the deadliest US tornado season in the last sixty years. As of April 2011, the storms of tornadoes have killed over 300 people in the Southern states of America. A tornado destroyed 75 percent of Joplin, Missouri, killing around 155 people, with some still missing at that time. The first two months of 2012, 115 tornadoes hit America, 55 percent higher than the average. Another tornado struck and wiped out the two Indiana towns of Henryville and Maryville, killing many people. The latest report is that more tornadoes hit Kansas the month of April 2012 than for the whole year. In December 2014, a tornado touched down in the state of Mississippi, very late in the season. In March 2015, tornadoes touched down in the Ozark Mountains of northwestern Arkansas and in Moore, Oklahoma, and killed two people. Several people were injured and and buildings sustained major damage, their roofs blown away. In April 2015, a tornado destroyed the small town of Fairdale, Illinois, killing two people and injuring eleven people, sweeping homes off their foundations. Also, tornado was on the ground in nearby town of Rochelle.

I've been through two tornadoes in my lifetime. The first one in 1948 hit in Coatesville, Indiana and near my home town of Danville. This storm done major damage plus killed one person, he was one of my junior high school class mates. The second one was on Palm Sunday 1965, which was near my hometown of Marion, Indiana. I was driving back from Fort Wayne, Indiana, and was within two miles from our home when I ran into this heavy hailstorm. This storm damaged my car, and I had to replace the roof on my home from the hail damage. Thank goodness there were no lives lost; mostly, it was heavy property damage to cars and homes. Driving around that town, I saw that many car dealers had been hit hard with hail damage, as well as damage to homes from the wind and many blown-down trees.

The first week of May 2015, in one day, fifty-one tornadoes touched down in four states of Kansas, Nebraska, Oklahoma, and Texas. Two days later, across the same plain states, there were eleven more storms. Oklahoma City area was hit the hardest with baseball hail and flooding and a few people injured, but no deaths. That same week, parts of Colorado were hit with big-sized hails, so thick they looked like snow on the ground. Mother's Day weekend of May 2015, a tornado hit Nashville, Arkansas, killing a young married couple in their trailer park. Their eighteen-month-old daughter survived. Also, in Van, Texas, this storm wiped out a third of this small town by destroying almost one hundred homes. This same weekend two dozen tornadoes ripped thru parts of five different states. It seem to be no end in the spring season of 2015, with so many tornadoes.

Floods in various places like Nashville, Tennessee of May 2010 and Minot, North Dakota, of June 2011 which done major damage. The flood of May 2010 in Bellevue, Tennessee, just west of Nashville caused major damage in the River Plantation condo addition. We lived within a half-mile distance of that major flood; it was so close to our home. Most of the people that lived in that condo addition were older retirees. They were saying, "It's going be hard at our age to start over again." With lots of prayers and helping hands from various church people, it became a double blessing in helping those in need. April 2015 saw heavy flood damage to Louisville, Kentucky, plus heavy rains in various parts of that state. May 2015 saw the worst flooding in history near Oklahoma City and Houston, Texas. This Texas city got eleven inches of rain in six hours. It was the wettest month of May on record for both Oklahoma and Texas. More than twenty other states were wetter than average for May.

The big super volcano for the USA might be coming someday. It will be the one under the Yellowstone National Park in Wyoming. If this super volcano erupted in the near future, the results would be unreal with unimaginable loss of lives and property damage. It was about 640,000 years ago that this volcano erupted. Yes, these are some of the signs of the end-times and the last days of this church age.

In May 1980, Mount St. Helens of Washington State erupted spreading ash, rocks, and hot gases into the air and causing mud flow down the mountainsides. Which cause 57 death from inhaling hot ash and damaged roughly 230 square miles of land around the mountain. The Ring of Fire is where 90 percent of the world's earthquakes and volcanic eruptions occur.

The Calbuco volcano in southern Chile erupted for three times in the last few days of late April 2015. This volcano has been inactivity for half century.

There have been several earthquakes around the world. These are just a few of them. In 1906, the Great San Francisco earthquake struck, killing an estimated 3,000 people and destroying 80 percent of the city.

In 1964, the largest recorded earthquake in US history (magnitude 9.2) struck Alaska, killing 120 people. Earthquakes are increasing in intensity every ten years, by double in numbers. The year 2004, it was the Indian Ocean Earthquake off the coast of Sumatra, Indonesia. The devastating tsunami killed over 230,000 people in fourteen countries, and the property damage was unreal, and so many people were left homeless for months.

From the years 2000 to 2010, there have been an estimated 425 major earthquakes of magnitude 6.0 or more around the world—such as Chile's mag. 8.8 earthquake, followed by New Zealand's magnitude 6.2 quake. In the year 2008, magnitude 8.0 quake hit the province of China, killing and injuring thousands of people; and in March 2011, Japan was hit by a 9.0 tragedy of quakes and tidal waves in what appears be a series of events accruing around the Pacific Ring of Fire. An earthquake hit in the middle of Virginia in August 2011, along with a severe tornado, all in one week. These are unheard-of situations for that area of our country. The fall of 2011, an earthquake hit near Oklahoma City. That year, the state of Oklahoma had 1,000 earthquakes, compared to the average of less than two hundred per year. In August 2014, Napa Valley, California, was hit by a magnitude 6.0 earthquake, the strongest in twenty-five years for that area. There are always lots of aftershocks from any earthquakes. Where will be the next major site? It might be Alaska or the West Coast of America. If so, the damage of property and the loss of lives would be unreal.

In April 2015, a super-great earthquake with a magnitude of 7.8 hit near the capital city of Kathmandu in Nepal, the worst in over eighty years. It was so powerful that it was followed with major after shocks of mag. 6.7 across the northern part of neighboring countries of Bangladesh, India, Pakistan, and Tibet. The total number of people killed was over 10,000, with many hundreds injured and still missing. Many were left homeless and living in tents; and there was a lack of food, medicine, power, shelter, and water, with hospitals full of injured people. Great deal property damage of homes and century old temples. Numerous countries around the world pledged immediate aid and supplies to this poor mountainous country. The USA sent U.S. Marines help with the rescue. Five days after the quake, miracles: a baby, a teenage boy, and a 101-year-old man were found still alive. The economy of Nepal, with population of 28 million people, is mostly tourism and mountain climbing. Near by is the largest mountain in the world, Mt. Everest, several mountain climbers were killed at or near the base camp from the quake. Three weeks later another earthquake of 6.3 magnitude hit again in this country, killing people with landslides and toppling buildings.

In April 2016, the country of Ecuador was digging out from its strongest earthquake in decades, that of 7.8 magnitude killing over 650 people and leaving thousands homeless. This happened just a few days after a powerful twin earthquake hit Japan, killing almost 50 people. Where will the next major earthquake hit again, maybe the western coast of America.? Such countries as these are part of the Ring of Fire for major earthquakes.

There has been a lot of talk regarding global warming. If this ever happened, there will be troubled times facing our America and other countries. Because of global warming, there will be melting icebergs, which will cause the ocean water to rise. This will cause major floods that will destroy cities along the east, gulf, and west coastlines of our nation, plus those places around the world. The global temperature for 2014 broke the previous record of the warmest years of 2005 and 2010 since record-keeping began in 1880. Overall, the USA had its thirty-fourth warmest year, with the worst being in the western states—those of California, Nevada, and Texas.

The last two winters of 2014 and 2015, the Midwest and Northeast states of our country were hit very hard with cold weather and lots of heavy snow. Some places in the Northeast states had record amount of snow and was bitter cold, like that of Boston, with over nine feet of snow and more on the way. This hard winter forced many businesses and the local-state government to shut down, and many schools were closed for days, or weeks. As of late February 2015, over seventy deaths across the country have been attributed to the very cold and snowy weather, which brought on mostly heart attacks while shoving snow and multicar pileups on several highways. In February 2015, both Crossville and Monterey, Tennessee, saw plenty of ice storm damage from up to one inch of ice; and schools were closed for two weeks. The people in these two towns were without heat, power, and water for several days; and many area churches came to the rescue with food and water, plus other necessary items. It was a major cleanup project for these two Tennessee towns, which lasted for weeks.

In January 2016, as one of the top ten snowstorms, Jonas, it hit eleven states. This snow storm went from Georgia, North Carolina, and Tennessee up to the Northeast states with blizzards, heavy snow up to three feet deep in places, and freezing rain. The hardest it cities were Baltimore, New York City, and Washington, DC. Most business places, government offices, and schools were closed for days. The results of this major snow storm that over twenty people had died, mostly from auto/truck crashes. According to a January writeup by USA Today paper that a study at Ball State University of Muncie, Indiana, the number of blizzards has doubled in the past decade. With that kind of news, we all should stock up on food and water as we bundle up by keeping warm with many more blizzards on the way for years to come.

Under these conditions, the American Red Cross is always there when families are wondering "What can I do now that everything of mine is destroyed?" The Red Cross organization is there no matter the situation—providing food, shelter, comfort, and hope. Take time today with your financial support or helping hand when or where ever there is a need.

Be in prayer, as our caring God is always there for people facing the unknown conditions with nowhere to turn in their lives in various storms, earthquakes, floods, hurricanes, and tornadoes that come across our country, as well as in other countries across the globe. Thank goodness that there are so many good charity organizations that are always there for many people in need.

14

THERE ARE MORE signs of the end-times or the last days. Let's take a look:

> "And there be famines and there shall be pestilence." (Matt. 24:7, Mark 13:8)

"Give us this day, our daily bread." Those are the needs of our hungry country and the starving world. In our country, the year 2015 has so far seen about 47 million people receiving food stamps. Thank you, Lord, for blessing the farmers and ranchers in the heartland of America, they are the ones that provide our daily bread. If it is true because of global warming, there will be a big shortage of food and water in our country and those around the world. We have great Christian organizations across our country providing necessary care, food, and water for the hungry and needy, these are some of them: Feed the Children (under the leadership of Rev. Larry Jones); the Second Harvest Food Bank of Nashville, Tennessee; Backpack Operation of Cookeville, Tennessee; Feed the Hungry by the LeSEA Broadcasting Networks; and Operation Blessing under Pat Robertson of CBN. The Baptist churches of Cookeville, Tennessee, provide food baskets to feed 20,000 people each Thanksgiving. The Cookeville Nazarene Church and the United Methodist Church in Bellevue, Tennessee, like so many other churches across the nation have a food bank. Several church ladies come in during the week passing out food to the needy and poor families. Let's keep those families in our daily prayers, and that God will bless those caring churches and the kindhearted people that are volunteering to help and serve.

If our God can feed the birds of the air and provide them nest for their daily rest, he can do much more for you and your family, for our good God is the same yesterday, today, and tomorrow. Just like the days of Moses's time of leading the people out of Egypt to the Promised Land. He provided bread from heaven and quail to feed 2 million people for forty years. This bread was called manna, and it tasted like wafers made with honey.

> Then the Lord said to Moses, "I will rain down bread from heaven for you. The people are to go out each day and gather enough for that day." The Lord said to Moses, "I heard the grumbling of the Israelites. Tell them, "At twilight you will eat meat,

and in the morning you will be filled with bread. Then you will know that I am Lord your God." (Exod. 16:4, 11–12)

Is it not to share your food with the hungry, and to provide the poor with shelter, when you see the naked, to clothe him. (Isaiah 28:7)

From the days of the early Pilgrims, who were celebrating a successful harvest with a feast in Plymouth Rock to the time of President Lincoln at Gettysburg, declaring a day of Thanksgiving by giving back to the less fortunate, it's a day of gratitude.

"For I was hungry and you give me something to eat, I was thirsty and you give me something to drink, I was a stranger and you invited me in, I needed clothes and you clothed me, I was sick and you looked after me, I was in prison and you came to visit me."

"I tell you the truth, whatever you did for one of the lease of these brothers of mine, you did for me." (Matt. 25:35–36, 40)

Let's be thankful for our farmers and ranchers across the heartland of America that feeds the world. About a hundred years ago 90 percent of our population were farmers. Now it's about 5 percent that are farming and ranching. Because of technology mechanization, our America and other countries around the world are producing more food than ever. We must pray for the starving world, that more food and safe water will be provided. America has the ability to feed most the world, yet our federal government pays farmers not to grow certain crops lest they glut the market and drive prices down. We need to improve this program as we are seeing the hungry children here in our land of America and the starving children in the rest of the world. Faithful believers based such operations from the book of Isaiah: "Feed the poor and clothe the naked."

We have a great God for He has blessed our farmers and ranchers so that they can feed the starving world. Today feeding the hungry people of our America makes me want to read again the Bible story how our Lord Jesus fed five thousand with five loaves of bread and two fish. Feeding five thousand men two thousand years ago was a gift from God. That same kind of gift is true today as our farmers and ranchers are feeding the people in our America and those people in other countries.

> When Jesus landed and saw a large crowd, he had compassion for them, because they were like sheep without a shepherd. So he began teaching them many things. By this time, it was late in the day, as the disciples came to him for the people were getting hungry. "How many loaves do you have?" he asked. "Go and see." When they found out, they said, "Five and two fish." Then Jesus directed them to have all the people sit down in groups on the

green grass. So they sat down in groups of hundreds and fifties. Taken the five loaves and the two fish and looking up to heaven, he gave thanks and broke the loaves. Then he gave then to the disciples to set before the people. He also divide the two fish among them all. They all ate and were satisfied, and the disciples picked up twelve basketfuls of broken pieces of bread and fish. The number of the men who had eaten was five thousand. (Mark 6:33-44)

Most Americans use about one hundred gallons of fresh water a day, while millions of people in other parts of the world use about five gallons of water each day. Some people in developing countries walk an average of four miles for one bucket of brown water. In our own country, we are seeing hot, dry climate changes; some of them are the following: In the year 2007, America's southeastern region experience the worst drought in more than one hundred years. For the last four years, a major drought in the southern Great Plains and mostly in the state of Texas, where ranchers lost crops and were forced to sell their livestock.

In the last few years, parts of California were seeing long, scorching dry spells, forcing farmers to drill deeper wells. As of April 2015, the state of California had its first mandatory statewide water restrictions because of shortage of water. There is a fine per day for overuse of water. The last four years, the drought has been hard on farmers and ranchers, forcing them to plow up their land that had grown various kinds of vegetables. The estimated idle acres is over a million as of springtime 2015, due to the drought. This is according to the University California–Davis. With the increasing world population, there will be a major shortage of water supply in some countries, and even in our own America. Someday in the future, science will, hopefully, come up with a way of using ocean saltwater as fresh drinking water.

According to a 2010 report by the federal government there are many signs of decreasing ground water levels across our country. The United States used 76 billion gallons of fresh water per day. Also, that sixty- four per cent of wells are draining dry. This will be a major concerned on farmers and ranchers due to lack of water as they feed the hungry and starving people of our country and rest of the world. Our country is one of the largest user of water in the world, others are China and India.

There is another concerned for the farmers and gardeners of America, bee population continue to slide. With fewer bees means less productive fruit and vegetables farms and fields. There seems little hope of a rebound anytime in the near future for bee population. This has been a unknown concerns for sciences for last few years of why the missing bees.

Our country and the rest of the world can take more lessons from Israel with the problem of water shortage. For many decades, Israel had droughts, than it figured out how to grow crops in the deserts. They are advising the world more than ever on how to manage scarce water resources. Israel are recycling used water, through desalination, plus better education. God is blessing His land of Israel as the New Garden of the World.

Our God in heaven always brings us showers of blessing each day, and he gives us living water just for the asking. Just like the story when Jesus was on a journey through Samaria, He rested by a well while his disciples went into a city to buy food. He asked a Samaritan woman for water.

The Samaritan woman said to him, "How can you ask me for a drink for you are a Jew and I am a Samaritan woman?"

Jesus answered her, "If you knew the gift of God who it is that asks you for a drink, you would have asked him, and he would have given you living water."

> "Everyone who drinks this water will be thirsty again, but whoever drinks the water I give him will never thirst. Indeed, the water I give him will become in him a spring of water welling up to eternal life." (John 4:9–10, 13–14)

She received the living water and immediately shared it, going into the city and inviting people to meet Jesus. There may be shortage of water in various places of America and around the world, but there is plenty of Living Water from our God in heaven. This Living Water can be a shower of blessing from heaven for you. Just ask for this, water and it's yours.

> He who oppresses the poor shows contempt for their Maker, but whoever is kind to the needy honors God. (Prov. 14:31)
>
> Is it not too share your food with the hungry and to provide the poor wanderer with shelter-when you see the naked, to clothe him, and not to run away from your own flesh and blood? (Isa. 58:7)

The Pacific Garden Mission of Chicago, Illinois, is the largest and oldest rescue mission in America, founded in 1877. This lighthouse mission can house up to 1,000 people per day, providing free food, clothing, housing, and dental and medical care. Also, they provide Christian counseling by pastors, getting the homeless and needy back on their feet. These pastors are there for the salvation of those who are seeking the Lord as their Savior. This mission, like so many rescue missions across our country, is a blessing in doing something for the homeless and needy. We have a rescue mission in my hometown of Cookeville, Tennessee, and what a great job they are doing. Under the leadership of both Rev. Larry Self and his wife, both retired, were serving their Lord for many years. This hometown rescue mission provides food, clothing, and shelter for men, women, and their children who need them. They have a thrift store that help with their expenses, plus money coming in from caring people and various charity organizations.

According to the Bible, the world is going get worse, not better. "And there be pestilence," better known as infection disease. The last few years, the United States has been stricken by pestilence and new infections. The deadliest pestilence in the world is HIV/AIDS. An estimate of 39 million souls have perished from this disease since 1981. Medical research is spending hundreds of millions of dollars in research for the cure of AIDS, Alzheimer's, cancer, diabetes, heart disease, and so many other health problems. Throughout the world, we are seeing the outbreak of cholera, malaria, and bird and swine flu, as well as the return of tuberculosis. Malaria is spread by the bites of infected mosquitoes. The year 2013, 198 million people were infected, and 500,000 died, most of them in Africa. Within the next year or two, the first ever vaccine for malaria will be available. February 2015, the Food and Drug Administration warned doctors and hospitals to use extra caution in the disinfection of hard-to-clean medical scope that has been linked to the spread of "superbugs" in outbreaks across the country. The scopes are used for a procedure with contrast dyes and X-rays to help doctors locate and treat blockage in the bile and pancreatic ducts.

In the year 2014, three countries in Western Africa suffered from outbreak of virus called Ebola, which was killing people by the hundreds monthly. There is other unknown disease that of Zika which is spread mostly by mosquitoes and that of sexual contact with people from those affected countries, which first appeared in the Western Hemisphere in May 2015. The outbreak has spread to over 25 countries and territories, including United States. The World Health Organization declared the rise of birth defects of infants born with blindness, smaller heads, and incomplete brain development that is link to the Zika virus. The latest report is that Zika virus is worsted than early forecast. According to a July 2016 report by FOX NEWS that there are 1,300 Zika-infected cases in our country, some of these are regarding defective born babies. Lord Jesus give us new hope and wisdom in the medical field for the right cured drugs against such as these cancer, Ebola, Zika, and so many others.

The biggest problem facing our country is people being overweight—about 45 percent of children and adults are obese. Such high obesity rate must be reduced soon. It's creating other future health problems, such as cancer, diabetes, and heart concerns. Thank goodness for medical research for controlling or eliminating the health problems of the past years, and doing greater medical research for the years to come. Help is needed in the form of financial support for organizations such as the American Cancer Society, the American Heart Association, and other organizations. Let's do our share in providing financial support so that people become healthier now and those in the future generation. I been doing my financial share with both the American Cancer Society and the American Heart Association for many years now. I have lost several members of my family over the years to cancer and heart conditions, and so have most of you.

Let me share with you all a story regarding my first wife who had colon cancer. It was the last of February 1993 when the doctors at Cookeville Hospital told us she had colon cancer, which was in the advanced stage. We drove to St. Thomas Hospital in Nashville for her treatments, a ninety-mile trip each way. By the end of May that year, the doctors told us, "This is the last treatment. We can't do any more. You have a few months to live. We will make plans for a hospice care for you." Believe me that was a long, silent trip back home. We shared the sad news with our three children; thank God they were very understanding. Her last request before she got really bad was to go back to Indiana to see her family and friends, go to our old church for Sunday services, and then stay a few days at the Turkey Run State Park, which was our favorite place for R&R. I took an early retirement in July from work to take care of her, till she died in October 1993.

Again, I will share with you a story regarding my oldest son:

My daughter picked him up and drove him to Bellevue, Tennessee, for us to have Christmas together. That night, he phoned me to tell me that they got back home safe and enjoyed the holiday. I did not call him that weekend for we were all together that Friday for Christmas. I received a phone call late Monday night that he had died. My guess is he passed away that weekend of a heart attack. He was only forty-seven. He was single and lived alone, and to die so young and so sudden. I was in charge of handling his estate, which was settled within five months in May 2010.

Again, I will share with you the story of my second wife's health condition. After having a knee replacement surgery, the next morning, which was Thanksgiving 2010, she had a bad heart attack, plus having low blood pressure at 70/45. She was in ICU for two weeks, and then was sent home under hospice care. I was her caregiver for the next four months till she died in March 2011.

I am sure that you all have similar health experiences with your loved ones. May the Good God bless you all.

Just like the days of Jesus time, this same Jesus is alive today and healing those who come to Him in faith.

We want to be healthy in our body, mind, and soul; but most important of all is our spiritual health, for our God is there for us. At times in our life, we maybe feeling bad or sick, but never say "Oh God, Why Me" and don't just give up. The Word of God is the very first place to go for our diagnoses. The God in heaven is our Great Medical Doctor for He has the healing hand and the healing power to heal your body, mind, and soul. All you need to do is ask in

Jesus's name, and you will receive your healing and all your needs; then you will be free.

Jesus came to heal those who need healing. There was the man with leprosy who became clean. He healed a paralytic who was able to walk again, the blind man at Bethsaida, the deaf to hear again, and he healed many who had various kinds of diseases. He also drove out many demons like the man who lived in the tombs that were always chained up.

> While Jesus was in one of the towns, a man came along who was covered with leprosy. When he saw Jesus, he fell with his face to the ground and begged him, "Lord, if you are willing, you can make me clean." Jesus reached out his hand and touched the man. "I am willing, and be clean." (Luke 5:12–13)
>
> Some men came, bringing to him a paralytic carried by four of them. Since they could not get him to Jesus because of the crowd, they made an opening in the roof above Jesus, and after digging through it, lowered the mat the paralyzed man was lying on. When Jesus saw their faith, he said to the paralytic, "Son, your sins are forgiven." (Mark 2:3–5)
>
> They went across the lake to the region of the Gerasenes. When Jesus got out of the boat, a man with an evil spirit came from the tombs to meet him. When he saw Jesus from a distance, he ran and fell on his knees in front of him. He shouted at the top of his voice, "What do you want of me, Jesus,

Son of the Most High God? Swear to God that you won't torture me!"

For Jesus said to him, "Come out of this man, you evil spirit!" (Mark 5:1, 6–8)

The story of a woman in a crowd who had a subject of bleeding for twelve years. When she heard about Jesus, she came up behind him in the crowd and touched his cloak. "If I just touch his clothes, I will be healed."

Immediately, her bleeding stopped, and she felt in her body that she was freed from her suffering. Jesus said to her, "Daughter, your faith has healed you. Go in peace and be freed from your suffering" (Mark 5:25–29, 34).

When Jesus again crossed over by boat to the other side of the lake, a large crowd gathered around him. One of the synagogue ruler, name Jairus, seeing Jesus for he fell at his feet and pleaded earnestly with him, "My little daughter is dying. Please come and put your hands on her so that she will be healed and live. So Jesus went with him. Some men came from the house of Jairus, "Your daughter is died," they said. "Why bother the teacher anymore." Jesus took the child's father and mother and the disciples who were with him and went in where the child was. He took her by the hand and said to her, "Little girl, I say to you, get up." Immediately she stood up and walked around. (Mark 5:21–24, 41–42)

Remember, that God is a God of miraculous, He can make a way for you. Miracles happen to those who believe, all you have to do is believe.

Our God is a healing God, for He is the same yesterday, today, and tomorrow for He never changes. whatever, whenever, and wherever you are, He is there for your needs. All you have to do is ask and you will receive. Thank you, Lord Jesus, for answering those prayers.

15

THERE ARE SO many other signs of the end-times or the last days of this church age. Some of them are as follows:

> "Brothers will betray brothers to death, and a father his child. Children will rebel against their parents and have them put to death. All men will hate you because of me, but he who stands firm to the end will be saved." (Mark 13:12–13)

The Spirit clearly states that in later times some will abandon the faith and follow deceiving spirits and things taught by demons.

> "Then shall they deliver you up to be afflicted, and shall kill you: and shall be hated of all nations for my name's sake." (1 Tim. 4:1)

Many Christians will become lukewarm in these end-times, and they really don't care what they are doing or saying. We need to have a powerful preaching of the Word of God during these troubled times. Let's preach that all the people be filled with the Holly Spirit. Now is the time for having a revival fire and say prayers for the unsaved. Let's put more kindle on those revival fires in Jesus's name.

> Multitudes who sleep in the dust of the earth will awake: some to everlasting life, others to shame and everlasting contempt. Those who are wise will shine like the brightness of the heaven, and those who led many to righteousness, like the stars forever and ever. Many will go here and there, to increase knowledge (Dan. 12:2–4).

There will be falling away of people in the end-times or the last days of this church age. We are seeing now many situations like this over the years in our America:

- Taking away Bibles and prayers in our school.
- Removal of Ten Commandments and "In God We Trust" from public buildings.
- Not allowed to say "God bless" or "Merry Christmas."
- Millions of abortions over the last forty years.
- Same-sex marriage.

Our country has seen an increase of knowledge in the last one hundred–plus years. These are a just few of them: The Wright Brothers' plane to the space age, horse and buggy to the fast transportation by cars and trucks, pony express to the Internet, printing press to computers, telegraph to cell phones, and the list goes on and on with progress. Yes, we are living in the fast lane of life. Maybe too fast, for we are seeing many busy people are doing this and that. Let's take time to "smell the roses of life." Take time to pray, take time to be with your family and friends, and take time to tell people about our Lord Jesus, and that we are living in the end-times and the last days of this church age.

> Many will go here and there to increase knowledge... Many will be purified, made spotless and refined, but the wicked will continue to be wicked. None of the wicked will understand, but those who are wise will understand (Dan. 12:4, 12:10).
>
> "Even so, when you these things happening, you will know that the kingdom of God is near. I tell you the truth, this generation will certainly not pass away until all things take happened. Heaven and earth will pass away, but my words will never pass away" (Luke 21:31–33).

Our big federal government are sowing seeds for our America's roots in rocky soil, all they are getting is briars, thistles, and tall weeds with thorns. This is why our nation is financial bankrupt with a broken down federal government. We need and want a government be sowing seeds of faith in black fertile soil for our America's roots. The final result will become a better and greater America. That is why in the Bible, our God want your faith be sowed in black rich soil, not rocky soil. That way your faith will have deep roots and grow deeper and greater in the Love of our Lord Jesus.

My Americans lets put our hands to the plow, lets be sowing seeds of faith for our country. Plow deep and wide that the faith seeds will have deeper roots, so our country can go forward being financial and military stronger as a world power country. We want a country that has Victory for our Lord Jesus, then He will Bless our America. We must obey His Ten Commandants by cutting out our sins in life, then the good Lord will give us a Blessing and Healing country.

> But the wisdom that comes from heaven is first of all pure; then peace-loving, considerate, submissive, full of mercy and good fruit, impartial and sincere. Peacemakers who sow in peace raise a harvest of rightness. (James 3:17–18)

We are engaged in a spiritual warfare every minute, every day with the Devil and his demons. God wants all Christians take a stand and be ready to win against those evil ones with the Sword of the Spirit and put on the full Armor of God, which is the Word of God.

Yes, it will happen again, but it be more worst when the three evil ones that of the Devil, the Antichrist, and the False Prophet are in controlled during the seven years of the Tribulation and the Great Tribulation periods. The whole world will become financially broken down; it will become the worst of all times for the unsaved people who took the mark of the beast of 666. However, God will take care of those believers that will become saved in Jesus's name.

We serve a God who will step out of the boat and calm the storms of today and those that may blow in tomorrow. He is a God that can say "Peace, be still" knowing we will be safe from all the storms that will be facing our America.

> The Lord your God is with you. He is mighty to save. He will take great delight in you, he will quiet you with his love, he will rejoice over you with singing (Zeph. 3:17).
>
> "Return to Me, with all your heart" (Joel 2:12)

16

THERE IS ONE more sign of Christ coming back for His church. It's the last sign of this church age as it's coming to an end. The Good News is that it's happened more so in this twenty-first century; the end of times is very near.

> "And this gospel of the kingdom will be preached in the whole world as a testimony to all nations, and than the end will come." (Matt. 24:14, Mark 13:10)

Our gospel preaching has come a long way. Years ago, it was the mission people with ham radios going into the jungles and the wilds of the world. Next came men of God known as the Circular Riders, preaching by horseback-riding from community to villages.

Around the turn of the last century, revival preaching and tent revivals with faithful men like Dwight L. Moody,

William "Billy" Sunday, Billy Graham, and Oral Roberts spreading the Good News of our Lord Jesus.

Rev. Dwight L. Moody once said, "I look upon the world as a wrecked vessel its ruin is neared and neared." God said to Moody, *Here is a lifeboat and rescue as many as you can before the ship sinks.* If the end-times seemed about to come in Moody's time (he died in 1899), how much closer must we be now? After 116 years from the time of Moody, the end-times, or last days, are very close. I can feel it, I can hear it, and I can see it a-coming.

Shortly after being saved through the outreach of the Pacific Garden Mission in Chicago, William "Billy" Sunday gave up his professional baseball career to work full-time for his and our Lord Jesus. Rev. Billy Sunday (1862–1955) became the best-known and most influential American evangelist during the first two decades of the twentieth century. Billy Sunday is still remembered today for his energetic preaching style and large successful evangelistic campaigns across the USA. In his lifetime, he preached to over 300 million people in the days before loudspeaker, radios, and television. These are the words from Preacher Billy Sunday: "I am an old-fashioned preacher of the old-time religion, that has warmed this cold world's heart for two thousand years."

Billy Graham started preaching in the late 1940s. They were the old-fashioned tent revivals. Billy Graham's first radio broadcast *Hour of Decision* began in 1950. Then in

1957, TV history was made when his NYC Crusade was held at Madison Square Garden life on TV. He was the Giver of God News. Rev. Billy Graham took God's words:

> "Go into all the world and preach the good news to all creation. Whoever believes and is baptized will be saved, but whoever does not believe will be condemned." (Mark 16:15–16)

This he did with his crusades in over 185 counties. Estimated total gatherings were at between 200 and 225 million people. Billy Graham preached by faith: "Commit your life to Christ," for God's Promise is true. As the choir sang "Just as I Am," people by the thousand came forward for their salvation during each of his crusades. Acts 2:21 tells us it shall come to pass that whoever calls on the name of the Lord shall be saved. Dr. Billy Graham has been a spiritual adviser to twelve American presidents, going back to the days of President Harry S. Truman to the present Forty-Fourth President. Now that he's retired, the good gospel is still being preached by his son, the Rev. Franklin Graham. Also, preaching is done by other family members of Billy and Ruth Graham. This whole family is blessed, and the believers are also bless for hearing the Good News from this faithful family of God.

Decision America Tour 2016 with Franklin Graham, son of Billy Graham, he will be preaching and leading prayer rallies in the Capitol cities of all fifty states. He is calling

Americans to believe the Gospel, repent from their sins, with many prayers, and live for our Lord Jesus Christ daily. God will use this Decision America Tour as a wakening up revival call for our nation. He believed the only hope for America is to have a whole wide nation revival, we must preach the Gospel like never before. My dear brothers and sisters in Christ, lets pray daily and help financial support for this last great cause. This maybe the last sign of revival fires before Christ come back in that big white cloud for His church.

After reading the third Epistle of John: Beloved, I pray that you may prosper in all things and be in good health, just as your soul prosper. Rev. Oral Roberts started the year 1947 with the ministry of healing, saving, and delivering the power of God. Rev. Oral Roberts conducted his ministry through faith healing crusades across the USA and around the world. Through the years, he has conducted more than 300 crusades on six continents, and laid hands in prayer on more than 2 million people. He is the founder of Oral Roberts University in Tulsa, Oklahoma. He was a pioneer in both radio ministry and the Abundant Life television revivals. His son, Richard Roberts, and wife Lindsey have taken over the ministry known as the Place for Miracles.

Starting with the year 2015, God has a new healing ministry for Richard Roberts. God wants him to minister to pastors and leaders, teaching them the three principles of healing, the Holy Spirit, and that of sowing/reaping.

He will become a minister to ministers teaching them the three principles of God. Also, for him to preach a stronger healing message on TV, plus continuing his healing school on the Internet. This means the word of God and that of His Healing Power is going out to the whole world. Yes, it means the end-times and last days of His church is now much closer. This is a bigger sign that our Lord Jesus is coming very soon. The Bible tells us to take the Gospel to the ends of the earth, sharing the good news of salvation and healing to all the people.

It's the faith of those early circuit rider ministry to the modern age of radio and TV ministry that we can hear and see the gospel being preached. Over sixty years ago, it was almost impossible to preach the gospel around the world. With this modern age of TV with the satellites in the heavens, it is now possible for the Good News be preached and taught around the world. With those satellites in heaven, it's like seeing our Lord Jesus putting His arms around the world with the gospel. Those end-times signs were being seen more so in the twentieth century, and now in the twenty-first century. You don't believe it, just read your daily news paper headlines or the see the nightly TV news of what is really happening in our world. Just start reading your Bible daily, for God is telling us that our Lord Jesus is coming soon for His church. I can feel it, hear it, and see it, that our Lord Jesus Christ is coming very soon for His church.

> "Therefore go and make disciples of all nations, baptizing them in the name of the Father and the Son and the Holy Spirit, and teaching them to obey everything I have commanded. And surely I am with you always, to the very end of the age." (Matt. 28:19–20)

Few years ago, my second wife, Nancy, and I made a trip to Scotland for the purpose of seeing where our family tree roots came from. That Sunday morning in our hotel room, I turned the TV on to hear and see a local church service. Imagine our surprise when we saw that it was The Hour of Power with Rev. Robert Schuler, all the way from California. Yes, the end-time days signs are now here; that gospel was being preached across America, then across the Atlantic Ocean, and finally into a hotel room in Scotland. Praise the Lord, Jesus is coming soon. This last sign is now. My dear brothers and sisters in Christ, be ready and watch out for the hour and time of our Lord coming for His church is very near. God's big clock in heaven is ticking away. That time might be high noon here in America, or somewhere else in the world it's the midnight hour.

The early TV Christian ministry of this country were the founders of Christian Broadcasting, such as Rev. Pat Robertson, Dr. Lester Sumrall, and Rev. Paul and Jan Crouch. We must keep on praying to keep Christian radio and TV ministry staying on the airwaves. Let's say "No more" and "Enough is enough" from any anti-Christian groups or the courts of our United States.

In 1960, Pat Robertson, with his young family and $70, took a giant step in faith, started the country's first Christian TV station located in Portsmouth, Virginia, and built it into CBN. God opened Pat Robertson's heart and gave him the command and directions that of "Be about the work of bring the Gospel to the nations. I want heaven filled with people who believe in My Son." It was his faith: "Command from the Lord to claim the airways from the Prince of Power of the air and give them to the Prince of Peace." Pat Robertson is the founder of the Christian Broadcasting Networks (CBN) and host of Christian TV program The 700 Club. There mission is to prepare America and the countries of the world for the coming of our Lord Jesus and the establishment of the kingdom of God on earth. His leadership for Operation Blessing and becoming president of Regent University in Virginia Beach is most rewarding.

Operation Blessing has been providing food, medical care, water, and various supplies to the needy throughout the world. Pat Robertson has been outspoken on conservative politics and evangelical Christianity in this country for many years. The good news is CBN is fifty-three years old as of October 1, 2011. As of 2016, CBN is broadcast in 149 different countries and territories of 38 different languages, plus an additional 29 languages on radio, the Internet, and by video. What a great outreach in these last days before our Lord coming for His Church. His son, Gordon Robertson, is following in his dad's footsteps in that CBN ministry. Praise the Lord, it will be going forward till Jesus comes for His church. The ministry of CBN will always be spreading the Gospel around the globe. I've been a financial partner for CBN's *The 700 Club* going back to the 1960s. Let's get involved together with financial support for Christian radio/TV ministry. We need it, and it's a must to keep those Christian radio and TV stations alive in Jesus's name. These Christians radio and TV stations are the final worldwide mission to preach the Good News that our Lord Jesus Christ is coming back soon for His church. My brothers and sisters in Christ, just keep looking up, for He is coming in that big white cloud.

In 1960, Dr. Lester Sumrall known as "the father of Christian TV," founded the LeSEA Broadcasting Networks located in Noblesville, Indiana, near Indianapolis. It is a multimedia network covering the globe to reach untold millions with the Good News. He dreamed of bringing the message of God's love and mercy to every country and nation. LeSEA operates television stations being broadcast throughout the USA, as well as in fifteen Middle Eastern countries. His vision is to "plow deep and wide" with the Good News and win a million souls for Jesus Christ every day. I met Dr. Sumrall through a full gospel businessmen meeting years ago at his TV station, and what a blessing knowing him and his sons, who are now doing the work of the Lord till Jesus comes for His church. Dr. Sumrall has a good blessing saying: "Feed your faith and starve your doubts."

In 1973, Paul and Jan Crouch co-founded the Trinity Broadcast Networks (TBN), which is located in Costa Mesa, California, and the Trinity Music City in Hendersonville, Tennessee. Under their leadership, TBN has grown to become our country largest Christian TV networks. TBN is viewed in other countries by seventy satellites and over 20,000 TV and cable affiliates. God is in control of the airways for Christian TV to reach out to the world with His Holy Word. Now his son Matt and wife are there helping with this TV ministry for it go forward when Jesus comes for His Church, Praise the Lord with the Good News. Yes, Jesus is coming soon, always be ready and watch.

It's because of the faithful leadership of these four people, and through their Christian Broadcasting TV stations and satellites that the world is hearing and seeing the Good News. The year 1977, the first satellite earth station seeing Christian ministry opened with the world to received the gospel of our Lord Jesus. The last sign for the end times and last days of the church age is NOW. I been financial supporting both Billy Graham and the CBN-700 Club for many years. These Christians TV Networks always need your financial support, please do it for our Lord Jesus.

We have come long ways in the last 2,000 years in the time of the healing, preaching, and teaching by Jesus. About three years later in His ministry, the church and the gospel got a bigger start when Jesus sends out the Twelve. Next, Jesus sends out the Seventy Two. Now, the Word of God is preached and taught around the world through radio and TV.

> Then Jesus went around teaching from village to village. Calling the Twelve to him, he sent them out two by two and gave them authority over evil spirits. They went out to preached that people should repent. They drove out many demons and anointed many sick people with oil and healed them.
> (Mark 6:6–7, 12–13)

Because of Christian satellite TV stations, the Word of God is carried around the world. It's a double blessing from God, which is almost like the Bible story of Elisha wanting a double portion of the Holy Spirit from Elijah. Let's take a look!

> Fifty men of the company of the prophets went and stood at a distance, facing the place where Elijah and Elisha had stopped at the Jordan. Elijah took his cloak, rolled it up and struck the water with it. The water divided to the right and to the left, and the two of them crossed over on dry ground. When they had crossed, Elijah said to Elisha, "Tell me, what can I do for you before I am taken from you?"

> "Let me inherit a double portion of your spirit."
>
> "You have asked a difficult thing," Elijah said, "yet if you see me when I am taken from you, it will be yours."
>
> As they were walking along and talking together, suddenly a chariot of fire and horses of fire appeared and separate the two of them, and Elijah went to heaven in a whirlwind. (2 Kings 2:7–11)

Yes, Elisha picked up the cloak that had fallen from Elijah and received both the double blessings from God and the double portion of God's Holy Spirit. God has blessed our America for so many years. Now it's up to us Christians to bless and please our God in heaven by spreading His Word around the world through the TV waves by means of satellites.

There is the urgency for worldwide mission work. Our God wants the message of the gospel to be spread around the globe. God's expectation is that we take the gospel to every creature more now than any other time. There is a world gospel mission headquarters known as World Gospel Mission located in Marion, Indiana. They help locate and provide financial support to Christian people going into the mission field. My family and I have lived in this area of Marion for over twenty years. I've been financially supporting this great mission WGM for several years in order that there will be a greater reach for worldwide gospel.

I enjoy hearing the Good News on Christian radio stations, my favorite is King of Kings Radio Network, WWOG 90.9 FM out of my hometown of Cookeville, Tennessee. This radio station provides gospel music and preaching around the clock every day of the year. From this radio station, I enjoy hearing the live true stories of the program *Unshackle* put on by Pacific Garden Mission out of Chicago. Telling the true stories of people going through some really hard times in their lives of drinking liquor, drugs, gambling, and stealing, which in turn caused marriage problems for them. Later, these people hearing the Good News at some church or at a rescue mission somewhere, they turned to God for their salvation. Hearing those great live stories that changed people's lives that has given them joy and peace in their hearts, minds, and lives. Some of those born again people went on to Bible college and later became ministers. Let's be saying "Praise the Lord" for this great Christian outreach.

Financial support is always necessary for the spreading God's Word around the world. My dear Christians, let's do more than our share. We need be working for His Church and for His Glory until the day of the Rapture. We don't want non-Christian people, our court system, organizations like ACLU and the federal government take radio and TV ministry off the airwaves. We must keep Christian radio and the TV ministry alive and have them as one in victory for our Lord Jesus. That time of His Coming for His church must be near. Just look around at what has happened to our country. Brothers and sisters in Christ, keep looking up, be ready, and watch for His Coming in the clouds. We must always have faith as believing Christians for the freedom and liberty, that we have a greater and stronger America. Now is the time for all faithful Americans to stand firm and tall in their Christian believes. Rekindle those revival fires; it's time for an old-fashioned revival from coast to coast across our America. Our God can and will turn our country around—only just start believing again. It's not too late. Pray that God will have mercy on our America and us Christians.

Be aware of organizations such as the American Civil Liberties Union, better known as ACLU. For many years, they've been one of the greatest threats to our freedom of religion. For years they have bullied businesses, colleges, schools, and individuals to adopt their views of America. They want take away God's word and prayer so that there be no more freedom of the press, freedom of religion, and freedom of speech. The ACLU is a very strong organization with their own attorneys, many members, and lots of money. Be aware of this ACLU organization. They are out to destroy our religions.

Because of violence against Christians in our country and around the world, many American churches are providing security systems for the safety of their members and staff. According to a December 2014 report by CBN, the Bellevue Baptist Church (30,000 members strong) of Memphis, Tennessee, is now providing security for their church members and staff. At various times on local TV news, there'd be a police report that someone had burned down a church or broken in to steal. It's hard to believe that we are seeing this in our own backyards of America, that anyone can be so mean enough to destroy God's house. This is why so many churches in our country lock their doors.

17

THE LAND OF Israel is the birthplace of the Jewish people. It's here that the Jews' political, religious, and spiritual identity was established. After being forcibly exiled from their land, the people kept their faith and never ceased to pray for the return to their land and for the restoration of political freedom. Israel signed their Declaration of Independence on May 14, 1948, the interim government of Israel took control. The first day of statehood for Israel was May 15, 1948. This was a day of Pentecost for them. After many hundred years, God's people are now in their land, and God will always bless their land. God promised his people in Israel that they will never move again. What a blessing of all blessings and a great understanding promise of all promises. America, let's be with Israel as partners all the time, whether it's good or hard times for them as their country is facing uncertain times with the world's countries against them. We must have faithful leadership in Washington DC to keep this faithful relationship alive between our America and the land of Israel.

> The Lord had said to Abram, "Leave your country, your people and your father's household and go to the land I will show you. I will make you into a great nation and I will bless you; I will make your name great, and you will be a blessing. I will bless those who bless you, and whoever curses you I will curse; and all people on earth will be blessed through you" (Gen. 12:1–3).

> They shall be my people And I will be their God, In truth and righteousness. (Zech. 8:8)

> "For I will take you out of the nations; I will gather you from the countries and bring you back into your own land. I will sprinkle clean water on you, and you will be clean; I will cleanse you from all your impurities and from all your idols. I will give you a new heart and put a new spirit in you; I will remove from your heart of stone and give you a heart of flesh. And I will put my Spirit in you and move you to follow my decrees and be careful to keep my laws. You will live in the land I give your forefathers; you will be my people, and I will be your God." (Eze. 36:24–28)

> "O Jerusalem, Jerusalem, you who kill the prophets and stone those sent to you, how often I have longed to gather your children together, as a hen gathers her chicks under her wings, but you were

not willing. Look, your house is left to you desolate. For I tell you, you will not see me again until you say, Blessed is he who comes in the name of the Lord." (Matt. 23:37–39)

God created Israel to be God's servant to be the "light to the nations." Israel was not to see itself as better than other nations, but as a tool of God's hand for the benefit of all nations. The people of Israel are God's chosen children.

But everything exposed by the light becomes visible, for it is the light that makes everything visible.

"Wake up, O sleeper, rise from the dead, and Christ will shine on you. Be very careful, then, how you live-not as unwise but as wise, making the most of every opportunity, because the days are evil." (Eph. 5:13–16)

Since 1967, the United States has supported Israel in economic, military, and political situations. In 1996, 2014, and again in 2015, the prime minister of Israel, Benjamin Netanyahu, warned that a nuclear Iran would be the greatest danger the world would face. This is God's Holy Land; God will only bless those nations that are good to His people and their homeland of Israel. Beware of any US president or any American secretary of state who wants to make policy changes in the financial, military, and political relationship between the USA and God's Holy Land. Our country has a good policy relationship with God's Holy Land since the days President Harry S. Truman signed the document that recognized Israel as a state. Christian people of our country, don't allow anyone to make any changes that would destroy this USA/Israel policy and keep our relationship alive by keeping it going forward. God will always bless those countries that bless Israel, and always curse those countries that curse Israel. This Israel is the center of the earth. God will see that this is always true. According to God, one king and one nation of Israel—no dividing of their land. To do this by our country, we will be seeing America blowing in the wind.

There is increasing criticism and demands from the United Nations for Israel to give up more land in pursuit of peace. Beware. If Palestine joins the United Nations, they would want a share of the land belonging to Israel and its capital city, Jerusalem. There is talk that Palestine wants the land of the West Bank. Be aware: this is God's land. America must be there and stand up for Israel during these troubled, uncertain times that they are facing in this twenty-first century.

Just few years ago our Forty-Fourth President met with the prime minister of Israel, Benjamin Netanyhu, over the issue between Israel and Palestine of building houses. This American president got mad over the outcome of this meeting. He did not have dinner with the prime minister or let him have a press conference. This prime minister went back home to Israel in disgrace over what our American president did to him. Sounds like a crying kid not getting his way, Mr. President, please take time to grow up and be wiser.

> I will make them one nation in the land, on the mountains of Israel. There will be one king over them all and they shall no longer be two nations or be divided into two kingdoms. They will be my people, and I will be their God. (Eze. 37:22, 37:23)
>
> "I will plant Israel in their own land, never again to be uprooted from the land I have given them." (Amos 9:15)

During these troubled times of the twenty-first century, we are seeing Israel's concerns about the need to defend themselves against the possibility of a nuclear attack from other countries, mostly from Iran. The USA is the only country or one of few that can help or come to the rescue for Israel. Our country must never forsake God's Holy Land of Israel and its people; otherwise, there will be God's judgment on this country or any other country.

Those early Pilgrims of the seventeenth century who landed on the eastern shores of the New World four hundred years ago, they built and put up a cross and got on their praying knees, thankful for their safe journey coming across the wide Atlantic Ocean. They were thankful for their new freedoms in the New World. This is our land, the USA. It was God who showed the Pilgrims the way to their/our Promised Land, the land of milk and honey. It was like it was hundreds of years ago that God showed the way for his people to their Promised Land, the land of milk and honey. America is our land, and Israel is their land, for He gave it to all of us.

The people of Israel have been traveling in the desert for thousands of years. It's the same with God's chosen people of Israel. This is their land, for God had shown the way. America will always be partners with the people of Israel. God will be there, as He always was, and show the way. During these end-times, or the last days, America might be Israel's only good friend and helping neighbor. Be aware, America, of what might be coming to us. Our own Forty-Fourth President has turned his back on Israel and its people several times. God will not bless any leader or country under such conditions. The prime minister of Israel came to America the spring of 2015 to address our US Congress. Guess who was not going to be there—the Forty-Fourth President and our own vice president, and the secretary of state. What does that tell you about anything, and a big *why*?

The Forty-Fourth President and some congressional Democrats are refusing to meet with PM Netanyahu for his speech at the US Congress on March 2015. The main reason is that it was an invitation from GOP House Speaker John Boehner without clearing the speech with the White House as diplomatic protocol. Also, another reason of not having their meeting it was two weeks before Israel election this was one reason according to the president. The number one reason is that the Forty-Fourth President doesn't like PM Netanyahu of Israel. This is one of many reasons why that God will bless any nation that will bless His Israel and curse any nation that will curse His Israel. Beware, my Christians friends and neighbors, of what is happening to our America, and why.

Is this one of the main reasons that our America has gone downhill from being a financial and military world power leader? We must always work together for a better relationship between our America and with God's Holy Land of Israel.

Israel has many names: Emmanuel Land, God's Holy Land, the Land of Milk and Honey, the Lord's Land, and the Promised Land. Yes, Israel is the Apple of God's eye. Israel is the center of the world, because our God is the center of the universe, and He holds the world in His hands.

There is no city like Jerusalem on the face of the earth. This Jerusalem is the city of God, the capital city of God, and the chosen city for His people. We must be praying for Israel each day—that our America keep Israel in our loving care as God kept His land in His loving care from the days of the old Promised Land of milk and honey to the present the twenty-first century as we wait for the New Jerusalem to come down from heaven.

Our America must always remember, that God only blesses those countries or nations that bless His Holy Land of Israel and curse those countries and nations that curse His holy land and His people. God has called us His children, to bless his Promised Land and its people. The last sixteen years of this twenty-first century, my question to you is, Are you seeing your America blowing in the wind because the president has turned his back on Israel?

Pray daily for greater peace for Israel, Jerusalem, and their people.

> "May those who love you be secure. May there be peace within your walls and security within your citadels." For the sake of my brothers and friends, I will say, "Peace be within you." For the sake of the house of the Lord our God, I will see your prosperity. (Ps. 122:6–9)

18

Is GOD TRYING to shake us or wake us up, that we are in the beginning days of sorrows? We are living in a world of wide financial crisis, disasters, earthquakes, famines, fires, floods, various storms, and terrorist around the world. Americans must and need be hearing with your ears and seeing with your eyes of what is happen around you. We need a spiritual revival in our country, thru prayer as God's children; He will give us a kinder heart for our America. God will humble His children as we believe in God's Word. Our America needs faithful men and women with good leadership in both the business world and our own federal government. My Americans, our big government, is not the solution to your problem, because having a bigger government is the problem. Only God is the answer, for He is the bridge over our troubled waters. Lord Jesus, reach down from heaven and touch our pleading hearts and praying hands, that we have a believing and faithful country. We must pray for our country, our communities, families, and especially our children and their children. They are the ones that will suffer the most. It's time to cry out, "O Lord Jesus Christ have mercy and hear our prayers; come into our life and give us new hope and peace of joy."

We are seeing bible prophecies rapidly being fulfilled each day of the year. Wake up my America before its to late. As we keep on going at this same sinful path, we are living in a time of no turning back for our America. We must turn to God and his word or our country will die. What does the word of God say? There is hope for America, that is His promise. All we need to do is turn back to God.

> If my people, who are called by my name, will humble themselves and pray and seek my face and turn from their wicked ways, then will I hear from heaven and will forgive their sin and will heal their land. (2 Chron. 7:14)

During these end-times, or the last days of this church age, we need to encourage each other. God's people should not fight one another over denomination and doctrines difference. When we all get to heaven, we all be one denomination—that is children of God. We are bound together by the shed blood of the Lord Jesus Christ. We are blood brothers and sisters in Christ. The church of our Lord should and will be as one body. The power of God will spread throughout the whole world if we only believe. Work for Christ and His church until He comes for His church. During our life span, we have special gifts, hands, mind, and talents. Let's make every day count as we all work together during His church age.

> Finally, be strong in the Lord and in his mighty power. Put on the full armor of God so that you can take your stand against the devil's schemes. For our struggle is not against flesh and blood, but against the rulers, against the authorities, against the powers of this dark world and against the spiritual forces of evil in the heavenly realms. Therefore, put on the full armor of God, so that when the day of evil comes, you may be able to stand your ground; and after you have done everything, to stand. Stand firm then, with the belt of truth buckled around your waist, with the breastplate of righteousness in place, and with your feet fitted with the readiness that comes from the gospel of peace. In addition to all this, take up the shield of faith, with which you can extinguish all the flaming arrows of the evil one. Take up the helmet of salvation and the sword of the Spirit, which is the Word of God. And pray in the Spirit on all occasions with all kinds of prayers and requests. With this in mind, be alert and always keep on praying for all the saints. (Eph. 6:10–18)

Thank you Lord for giving our country so many churches, that we can go to any church of our choice. Whatever the denomination, there is a church for you and your family. You have this right according to the US Constitution and the Declaration of Independence; this is called freedom of religion. By radio and TV we can hear and watch any Christian program of your choice. Stand firm and tall, my American friends. Don't let the courts or the anti-Christian people take away radio or TV Christian programs off the air, such as *The 700 Club* with Rev. Pat Robertson, *Breakthrough* with Rev. Rod Parsley, Cornerstone Church with Rev. John Hagee, *The King Is Coming* with Dr. Ed Hindson, *The Bible Prophecy* with Dr. Jack Van Impe, *Bible Prophecy Revealed* with Grant Jeffrey and Rev. Perry Stone, *Turning Point* with Dr. David Jeremiah, and positive Christian uplifting with Rev. Joe Osteen, and so many others. They are preaching the Good News of Christ coming for His church. We need to put our trust in our God during these difficult times, so we can still be happy and believe in the good things. Financial support is needed for both Christian radio and TV stations to stay on the air. When I travel by car, I always listen to a Christian radio program. My favorite local radio station is that of King of Kings, 90.9 FM WWOG, out of Cookeville, Tennessee/Somerset, Kentucky, or 1300 FM Christian radio station out of Nashville, Tennessee.

Our churches across this nation need good, faithful Bible preaching to uplift people's spirits. I have heard there is a shortage of people going into the ministry. This must change for the sake of our young generation and the future generation. Church attendance began to change in the 1960s and the trend has not reversed in the twenty-first century. According to a Gallup survey, church attendance between the years 1991 through 2013, the percentage rate is between 40 to 49. Only the state of Utah has church attendance just above 50 percent; only three or four Southern states have church attendance in the upper 40 percent. Going to church is not as important to Americans as it used to be. Some denominations have seen their membership shrink almost in half since the 1960s. The smaller churches in various communities and villages with less than fifty people in attendance are facing difficult times keeping the church doors open. There are many cases where a minister has two or three small churches for each Sunday service. Those financial burdens are on the backs of older people, as the younger people went on to bigger towns and cities for better jobs. With daily faithfulness in God's Word, we will find strength for today and a brighter hope for tomorrow. God wants His church be one that is alive and one in victory for our Lord Jesus, keep up your good works up to the time of His coming for His church.

Here in Cookeville, Tennessee, there is the Tennessee Bible College. They are starting a new class aimed to train more preachers. This class started because they were getting many phone calls from churches that needed preachers. At times is take up to an year or more to find a preacher for a church, this seams so unreal in this time. This class is under the leadership of Rev. Kerry Duke, he is vice president of TBC and the senior pastor of West End Church of Christ located in Livingston, Tennessee. Thank you, Rev. Duke, for your concern and leadership for finding future ministers.

We are seeing more sports events on Sunday than any other time in the past years. Even some churches are having early-morning services, so people can go and watch their favorite ball game or team. America, what is more important, going to God's house or going to a sports stadium to see a ball game? The last several years, we are seeing malls and shopping centers open on the Lord's day, many stores open every day of the year except for Thanksgiving and Christmas. It's all because of the mighty dollar for the owners and the stockholders! Sunday should be a day of rest and for going church with your family.

These are troubled times in our land. This is the reason for an old-fashioned church revival to up lift our country. God is the only answer for these trouble times that is facing our country. Now is the time for all believers get on our praying knees, that God will have mercy for our country. We are praying for your forgiveness and mercy for the sins in our land.

19

AT THIS TIME, I want to introduce to the readers my two best friends in Christ—a dear minister and his charming wife, Rev. Frank Bunn and Mary Ellen Bunn. Their church is located in New Maysville Community Church, New Maysville, Putnam County, Indiana.

Preacher Frank and Mary Ellen were in their late eighties and still active doing God's work each Sunday morning church services, Sunday evening services, and Wednesday evening Bible study. His background was first as youth minister and later as senior pastor preaching and teaching the Good News of our Lord Jesus over fifty years. Their ministry had been in smaller churches that are located in both Hendricks and Putnam County, Indiana. He had a powerful Lord's message each Sunday morning and evening services. He would always end his sermon with saying "Keep looking up." No white wash sermons from this preacher, he told it like it is.

The summer 1999, my second wife, Nancy, and I went to Danville, Indiana, for my 1953 high school class dinner/reunion that Friday evening and the all high school class dinner/reunion Saturday evening. That Sunday morning, while driving to visit with my cousins, the Cloncs family and the Gross family in Roachdale, Putnam County, Indiana, I told my wife, Nancy, we are going to turn here at Groveland and go to the cemetery where my mother is buried. We arrived at this small farming community of New Maysville and passed a white-frame country church. I looked at my watch. It was 10:00 a.m. We always stop for church somewhere as we travel. Being the only church in town, this was the must stop for us to go to church services that Sunday morning. This farming community was founded in the 1830s. Now the population has gotten smaller as people moved to cities and larger towns for better jobs.

We went on to the cemetery. I have three generations of my mom's family buried there: my mother, Rebecca Ruth Sheckles Robertson; her sister Mary Sheckles Gross; their parents, Charles and Alvora Surber Sheckles; their grandparents, James and Alvora Sheckles; and their other grandparents, William and Lydia Eggers Surber.

Then we went back to the New Maysville Community Church for morning services. We introduced ourselves, told them we had been to the cemetery, and that I had family roots in that community. What a welcome we got! The preacher and his wife wanted us to go home with them for lunch, but we had other plans for our family dinner/reunion. Each year, when we make our Indiana trip, we always went back to the New Maysville Community Church seeing our caring new church family.

On the way home, we always take time to stop for a nice visit of sharing time with Preacher Frank and Mary Ellen at their lovely country home. They would call us the next morning, making sure us "kids got home safe." That makes you feel good that you are part of that church family. My dear friend and man of God, Preacher Frank Bunn, died in January 2012. Mary Ellen died the spring of 2014. They will be missed there in the Hoosier State as the Preacher of God. Jesus will be saying to Preacher Frank and his wife, "Welcome to your heavenly home, for you are now in the hands of your Lord. Well done, my faithful son and daughter." This small country church is still alive and preaching the Good News. My dear friend Rev. Larry Edwards is the new pastor at the New Maysville Community Church, and he knows how to preach the Word of God.

Like so many small community churches across our country, the New Maysville Community Church had its first Lord's Day in July 1839. This church's doors are open with life, light, and love for the fulfilling of God's Word. Over the years, the men remodeled the inside of the church and ten years ago build a fellowship addition with class rooms and kitchen to the old church building. This church is built on solid rock for people hearing the Good News. Our Lord Jesus wants His church be one that is alive and has victory for His people. This small country church is like the church in the ole song

> There's a church in the valley by the wildwood,
> no lovelier ever spot in the dale;
> no place is so dear to my childhood,
> as the little church in the vale.
> How sweet on a clear Sunday morning,
> to list to the clearing bell;
> its tones so sweetly are calling,
> Oh, come to the church in the vale.
>
> "Do not be afraid little flock, for your Father has been please to give you the Kingdom." (Luke 12:32)

Thankful to our great God, for He has given our country so many different denominations that people can find a church for their spiritual needs. I have heard that there are 275 different denominations, so there is one for you and your family. What is most important is to find a Bible-preaching and Bible-teaching church that you and your family feel comfortable with. Parents with children, a Sunday school and summer vacation school is a must for teaching the young ones the Word of God. The future of the church is in the hands of the little children. They are the Christians for tomorrow. The family is important. It was God's idea in the first place, with the first family being that of Adam and Eve. The family, the home, and the church are the places where good values are made clear, goals are set, and integrity is formed. Read your Bible daily, pray daily, be with your family daily, and go to church each Sunday as a family.

Churches come in all sizes, with weekend attendance such as these. Just find one that you like as a family:

> Attendance kinds
>
> More than 2000—mega church
> 301 to 2000—large church
> 100 to 300—medium church
> Less than 100—small church

Majority of the small churches across our country have Sunday attendance of one hundred or less people, they are located in cities, small communities, and towns. There are advantages for finding a medium or small size church for yourself or your family. The following are just a few of those advantages, just follow your heart, mind, and spirit; they will led you to that certain church. The final results are that you and your family will receive that special blessing from the Holy Spirit.

- You get to know everybody by name or by sight, sense of belonging.
- There is a greater awareness of needs, such as financial, medical, spiritual.

- The church minister, pastor, or priest can truly shepherd his sheep, which is a must for all churches.

Since we are living in the end-times, or last days, of this church age, finding and going to church is a real must. People who are homebound or in nursing homes, there are so many radio and TV Christian programs for your needs and wants. Thankful for church members, their families, and friends taken time for visiting with people in nursing homes. This is a great ministry of visitation. Just take some time, that you do care and are concern for those Golden Age people. My lady friend Wilma Hayes and I always take time to visit with people at rehab centers and nursing homes, and seeing special-needs people such as those with Alzheimer's and our special mental/physical friends at Pacesetters. Just take time to be a good friend and neighbor to these people. They like to be loved and to know that someone loves them.

If you are in the neighborhood of Putnam County, Indiana, there will be a big Christian welcome for you by the New Maysville Community Church of "Come on in to God's House." You can hear the Good News from the Word of God, communion, music with singing, and praying time—all that is there for you. Always as you travel with your family, stop somewhere for church of your choice because our God is there for you. Yes, even as you're driving to work or going back home, a Christian radio program will give you peace of mind after a hard, long day. The Good

News is there for your family as you go to church and that of hearing gospel music and preaching on Christian radio and TV stations always brings much joy and peace for your body, mind, and soul.

20

Beware, my dear Americans, our nation is heading toward socialism, seeing our nation's big federal government becoming bigger but not better. Yes, the day is already here that Big Brother is watching you. We can't go to any bank or store in America with so many cameras seeing what you are doing or where you are.

It's the free business enterprise that drives the nation, not bigger government. Over 70 percent of the consumers and the small businesses on Main Street of America are what financially support our country. Our federal government is spending money or writing checks with no money in the bank. That is spending money on borrowed money that is also borrowed. The time is coming very soon for the death of the American dollar being replaced with another world currency, then we will be seeing much higher inflation and taxes. Do you want see our America blowing in the wind?

Lord Jesus, reach down from heaven and hear our pleading hearts and touch our praying hands. Give us a country that can go forward with lots of freedom, liberty, and victory.

We are living in prophetic times, Jesus Christ will soon be returning for His church. The Lord of Lords, King of Kings wants a church that is glorious, victorious, and a winning one. Also, our Lord wants the same for our America, one that is glorious, victorious, and winning.

> Many will see and fear the Lord and put their trust in the Lord. (Ps. 40:3)
>
> In the last days, God says, I will pour out my Spirit on all people. Your sons and daughters will prophesy, your young men will see visions, your old men will dream dreams. And everyone who calls on the name of the Lord will be saved. (Acts 2:17, 2:21)

The goal of the church is to spread the loving power of God's living word throughout the world. Next, the church wants each person to be born again or saved in the spirit of our Lord Jesus. It cannot be done without love. Because love never, never fails. What beautiful words from God, and they are all true, mostly the word of love.

> And now these three remain: faith, hope, love, but the greatest of these is love. (1 Cor. 13:13)

Rev. Frank Bunn had a phrase: "Keep looking up." What does that mean for you and our America? When I go outdoors each day, I am looking up in the sky to see the clouds. Some days the sky is blue, sunny with some or no clouds. Other times, the sky is very cloudy, showing signs of rain or snow. I am looking for that special blue sunny sky day with a certain big white cloud, the one that Christ be coming on for His church. Brothers and Sisters in Christ always be ready and watch, keep looking up for that day of His coming because it is sooner than soon. We may not know the day, hour, or the time; its closer for that time as we approach high noon or the midnight hour for His coming for His church. Now is the time for all the churches of our nation, for all the pastors, preachers, and priests to be preaching what the people *need* to hear, not what they *want* to hear. Members of the church and people of this world are starving for the soul food of God's Word and thirsty for His holy living water of the Good News. Keep looking up for that big special white cloud that is coming in with our Lord Jesus.

> Who also said, "Men of Galilee, why do you stand here looking into the sky? This same Jesus, who has been taken from you into heaven, will come back in the same way you have seen him go into heaven." (Acts 1:11)

As that great gospel song, "Because He Lives" goes, "I can face tomorrow / because I know He holds the future."

Lord Jesus, take my hand. Don't let me stand alone. My dear brothers and sisters in Christ, just take one step forward, for our Savior is there for you and me. He will take our hands and take us all the way to heaven.

> Brothers, we do not want you to be ignorant about those who fall asleep, or to grieve like the rest of men, who have no hope. We believe that Jesus died and rose again and so we believe that God will bring with Jesus those who fallen asleep in him. According to the Lord's own word, we tell you that we who are still alive, who are left till the coming of the Lord, will certainly not precede those have fallen asleep. For the Lord himself will come down from heaven, with a loud command, with the voice of the archangel and with the trumpet call of God, and the dead in Christ will rise first. After that, we who are still alive and are left will be caught up together with them in the clouds to meet the Lord in the air in glorified bodies. And so, we will be with the Lord for ever. Therefore encourage each other with these words. (1 Thess. 4:13–18)

> By his power God raised the Lord from the dead, and he will raise us also. Listen, I will tell you a mystery: We will not all sleep, but we will all be changed in a flash, in the twinkling of an eye, at the last trumpet. For the trumpet will sound, the dead

will be raised imperishable, and we will be changed.
Death has been swallowed up in victory.
(1 Cor. 15:15, 15:51–52, 15:54)

"Two men will be in the field; one will be taken and the other one left. Two women will be grinding with a hand mill; one will be taken and the other one left. Therefore keep watch, because you do not know what day your Lord will come." (Matt. 24:40–42)

God's big clock in heaven is ticking. The time is almost high noon here in America, or somewhere else in the world, it's closer to the midnight hour. Brothers and sisters in Christ, always be ready and watch for the time is nearer when Christ will be coming . Be aware, my America, for we are living in the end-times or last days of His church age. That time is like the spring planting season for finding the unsaved people, and then later it will be the harvest autumn season time getting to be born again or the saved people ready for the Rapture. Each one of us knows an unsaved person. It might be a loved one or a friend; such a person needs salvation. During these uncertain times, church revival is a must for saving the unsaved so they can be with the Lord Jesus in heaven. Let's rekindle those ole revival fires in the name of Jesus Christ. He is our Lord and Savior. Our America must be more faithful now during these uncertain times. Let's always be ready and watching before God's calling for His church.

> Now, brothers, about times and dates we do not need to write to you, for you know very well that the day of the Lord will come like a thief in the night. You are all sons of the light and sons of the day. But since we belong to the day, let us be self-controlled, putting on faith and love as a breastplate, and the hope of salvation as a helmet. For God did not appoint us to suffer wrath but to receive salvation through our Lord Jesus Christ. He died for us so that, whether we are awake or asleep, we may live together with him. Therefore encourage one another and build one another up, just as in fact you are doing. You ought to live holy and godly lives and look forward to the day of God and speed its coming. (1 Thes. 5:1-2, 5:5, 5:8-11; 2nd Pet. 3:11)
>
> No one knows about that day or hour, nor even the angels, nor the Son, but only the Father. Be on Guard! Be Alert! You do not know when that time will come. (Mark 13:32–33)

Always be ready, waiting, and watching. Christ will be coming for His Church sooner, than soon. Be ready with the full armor of God as a soldier in God's army, waiting with the faith in Christ, and watch with the peace of Christ. My Christian brothers and sisters in Christ, put on your breastplate of love and the helmet of salvation, we are in God's army of winning souls. Let's be standing firm and tall for our Christian Believes as we march of keeping in step for we are in the army of our Lord Jesus. He is our Commander in Chief all the way from heaven.

Some people today are trying to change the history of America by leaving God out of our country, but the truth is, God has been part of this nation before its beginning. He still wants to be, and he always will be, part of our country, if we only turn away from our sins and start believing again. Always be in prayer for our country, that God will keep on blessing this land of ours. Otherwise, we will be seeing our America blowing in the wind.

The people of our America are hungry for God's Soul Food, His Word, and thirsty for God's Living Water. Its time for the Church get on their knees in prayer, our country is in need for a coast to coast revival. There is no time for the church to be sitting on their hands, and none of this whitewashed sermons. During these end-times, or last days, of His church, let's be getting more people saved before it's too late. People of America, we should always be working for Christ during our working lifetime, and also during our golden retirement years. Always be working for His church until the good Lord comes for you and for His church. Our Lord Jesus wants His church be alive and His church with the gospel of Victory, just like in that old song "Victory in Jesus."

Let's sing together that old gospel song "Grace Alone."

> Every promise we can made,
> Every prayer and step of faith,
> Every difference we will make only by Grace.
> Every mountain we will climb,
> Every ray of hope we shine,
> Every blessing left behind,
> Is only by His Grace."

Grace alone, which God supplies, strengthens the unknown of our daily life for He will provide for all our daily needs all the time. Having Christ in our life for He is our cornerstone and foundation, He will build our homes and our lives on solid rock. Likewise, we want a federal government to be built on solid rock, not one built on sand.

> "Ask and it will be given to you; seek and you find; knock and the door will be opened to you. For every one who asks receives; he who seeks finds; and to him who knocks, the door will be open." (Matt. 7:7–8)

The churches of this twenty-first century, must always keep their doors open for those who are asking, seeking, and knocking. I believe that our Messiah, Jesus, wants us to be informed of current events, what is happened in the many parts of the world, including our own America. We must be reading the Bible each day. It tells the future of our country and for our lives. His church will be removed from this earth in the Rapture, and the believers will be saved from the wraths that are yet to come. The Christians who have trusted Christ as their personal Lord and Savior will escape the Tribulation.

> We live by faith, not by sight (2 Cor. 5:7)
>
> "All authority in heaven and on earth has been given to me. Therefore go and make disciples of all nations, baptizing them in the name of the Father and to the Son and to the Holy Spirit, and teaching them to obey everything I have commanded you. And sureely I am with you always, to the very end of this age." (Matt. 28:18–20)

The Prophet Amos said, "Prepare to meet God." Are you ready to meet God?

No excuses, for the time is getting shorter. Now is the time for you get involved in God's work.

> "Enter through the narrow gate. For wide is the gate and broad is the road that leads to destruction, and many enter through it. But small is the gate and narrow the road that leads to life, and only a few will find it." (Matt. 7:13)

Repent of your sins. Receive Christ as your Lord and Savior. Christ will forgive your sins, and you will receive a new meaning for your life, with new aims, new dimension, a new heart and mind, and new objectives, and you will begin a new relationship with God with a brand-new life.

It will be like that old song "Give me that old-time religion / it's good enough for me."

We never walk alone, for Christ walks with us. The good Lord will take your hand in His hand, He will never let go of your hand. Just a closer walk with Him. Thank you, Lord Jesus, for hearing our prayers and wiping away the tears in our eyes. Do I hear, a "Praise the Lord" for your decision of your new life? We are His children. He knows our needs. Just trust in Him.

Dwight D. Eisenhower, better known as Ike, and who was a general in the US Army during World War II and later became president of the USA, stated these words of faith and wisdom: "There are no atheists in foxholes."

If you are in a foxhole or going through dark storms, God will get you out of those foxholes of life. If you are in a dark storm of life today, God will provide peace and safety for you during those troubled times in your life.

The National Day of Prayer is an annual observation held on the first Thursday of May, inviting people of all faith to pray for our country. It was created in 1952 by joint resolution in the US Congress and signed into law by President Harry S. Truman. Year 2011 was the sixtieth annual National Day of Prayer with the theme "A mighty fortress is our God." Be aware of any American president who does not want a National Day of Prayer. He may not be a believer in our Lord Jesus. Just pray for such American President or any leader that they may see the Light.

The year 2015 will be the sixty-fourth anniversary for the National Day of Prayer, and the theme is "Lord, hear our cry" and is based on the following from the Bible: Here in Cookeville, the services will be at the Putnam County Courthouse on the south lawn on May 7 with praise, worship, and with prayers by local church pastors.

> Yet give attention to your servant's prayer and his plea for mercy. O Lord my God. Hear the cry and prayer that your servant is praying in your presence this day. (1 King 8:28)
>
> The Lord is my rock, my fortress and my deliverer, my God is my rock, in whom I take refuge. He is my shield and the horn of my salvation, my stronghold. (Ps. 18:2)

Prayer has always been used in this country for danger, protection, and strength, even before we were a nation. Prayer was used by the Pilgrims as they got on the shore of the New World. Prayer was used in 1776 by our Founding Fathers. Prayer was used by President Abe Lincoln during the Civil War. Prayer was used by President Franklin D. Roosevelt during World War II, and so many other faithful praying Presidents. The year 2011, the Forty-Fourth President canceled the National Day of Prayer, not having the Rev. Franklin Graham attend for his message from God. How sad for such a condition. This is another new sign that our great country is losing our Freedom and Liberty.

Our America needs God for a believing country and that He will give back to our America a God-fearing president who will lead our America in Victory. This President is misleading and not leading our country, he has turned his back on Israel many times and will do it again. God will bless those nations that bless His holy land and His people, and curse those nations that curse His holy land and his people. My America, is this what has happened to our America of this twenty-first century that we are being deceived by our forty-fourth president?

> "Now when these things begin to happen, look up and lift up your head, because your redemption draws near." (Luke 21:28)

We don't know when Christ will return, but we do know that He will come again. The Bible says only the Father in Heaven knows the exact date of the Savior's return. Until that time, we should be living godly lives on this earth, waiting and working until Jesus comes for His church. Come, Lord Jesus, we are watching and waiting.

> He who testifies to these things says, "Yes, I am coming soon." Amen, Come, Lord Jesus. The grace of the Lord Jesus be with God's people. Amen. (Rev. 22:20–21)

The writer has finished the second part of this book, regarding the end-times or the last days of His church age as we wait for the Rapture of God's church. We are going home in heaven with the Lord. It's like going on a trip with young kids in the back seat of the car saying, "Are we almost there yet?" Yes, we are almost home. Jesus will be there on the front porch of your new home in heaven, with the red-carpet treatment, saying, "Welcome home, my faithful brothers and daughters."

Always be working for the Lord up until the Rapture of His church. Be ready and watch for that hour is near. God's big clock is ticking, for its high noon here, and somewhere else it's the midnight hour. Christ will come like a thief in the night when you are not watching, so always be alert and be ready for the coming of His church. Keep looking up. Christ will be coming in the clouds to take His church home.

21

Days after the Rapture

THE FINAL PART of this book covers the time after the Rapture of God's church. Most of this information is taken from the Book of Revelation; others were taken from the Bible with references as noted.

The church with the believers are now safe in heaven, rejoicing with gladness and much joy. They are safe in their heavenly home and being with their Lord Jesus. However, those left behind on earth are going through confusion over what has happened. There will be times of protesting and riots for food and other necessities. So many key Christians are now gone; people in need of medical attention are made to wait and are given very little aid. Those unsaved people will see seven long, hard years ahead of them known as the Tribulation and the Great Tribulation. Yes, there will be breaking news on all radio stations and TV channels, day and night. What happened? Where are the missing people? Lots of *what*, *when*, *where*, and *why*.

Those people left behind after the rapture can be saved, but with difficulty. However, there will be many that will have hardened hearts and minds, that will never change. The current crisis here in America and around the world is forcing the nations of the world into a One World Order. This One World Order involves the elimination of the independence and sovereignty of nations, states, and some form of world government. This means the end of America and what it stands for—that the United States Constitution, the Declaration of Independence, and the Bill of Rights, as we know them, all will be gone. There will be no middle class of people, only rulers and servants. All laws will be uniform under a legal system of World Courts. The death of the US dollar creating both a World Bank and a new world currency. There will be a New World Order of Religion under the control of the False Prophet. Gone are those times when you can hear such words as "In God we trust," "praise the Lord," "Merry Christmas," and many others. During the time of the seven-year tribulation, the world will see the government at its worst, a One World Government under the control of Satan the devil.

Shortly after the Lord Jesus comes to take His Church to Heaven, there will follow a period of seven years known as the time of Tribulation. This seven year period is also known as Daniel's 70 Weeks. This is a week that consists of not seven days but seven years. The last three and half years is often called the Great Tribulation because it will be the greatest and worst of troubled times the world has ever known.

> "For then there will be great distress, unequaled from the beginning of the world until now, and never be equaled again" (Matt. 24:21).
>
> Come up here, and I will show you what must take place. (Revelation 4:1)

In the revelation of Jesus Christ, which God gave Him to show his servants what must soon take place, He made it known by sending his angel to his servant John. The book of Revelation was written around the year AD 96 by John the Apostle or John the Revelator through a vision during his exile in the Island of Patmos, off the coast of Turkey. John was preaching the Gospel with such power and the Spirit that he was exiled to Isle of Patmos. The book of Revelation centers around symbols and visions of the Resurrected Christ, who alone has authority to judge the earth, to remake it and to rule it to rightness.

"Write, therefore, what you have seen, what is now and what will take place later" was the word of God to John.

> And I saw a mighty angel proclaiming in a loud voice, "Who is worthy to break the seal and open the scroll?" (Revelation 5:2)

> But no one in heaven or on earth or under the earth could open the scroll or look inside. I wept and wept, because no one was found worthy to open the scroll or look inside. "Do not weep! See the Root of David, he has triumphed. He is able to open the scroll and its seven seals." (Revelation 5:3–6)

The wrath of God will be hard and tough, consisting of three main judgments of seven each. They are the Seal Judgments, the Trumpet Judgments, and the Bowl Judgments. Only the Lamb is worthy to open the seals of the scroll of the Seal Judgment.

The Book of Revelation tells of a scroll in God's right hand that is sealed with seven seals. The first four seals are the Four Horsemen of the Apocalypse.

> I watch as the Lamb open the first of seven seal. Then I heard one of the four living creatures say in a voice like thunder, "Come!" I look and there before me was a white horse, its rider held a bow and he was given a crown, and he rode out as a conqueror bent on conquests." (Rev. 6:1-2)

A man on a white horse, with a bow and a crown, who is a conqueror; this is the Antichrist. This evil one will be going here and there, conquering only with a bow without any arrows. The bow is a sign of military power. Such a evil person must be a great spokesman of many words, deceiving people by the millions upon the whole wide world. This evil one will come preaching peace, many will believe and follow him. Also, he will claim to be God, people will believe this evil one. This evil one will be preaching and teaching false religion or different cults. He is called by many names: the Antichrist, the Beast, Man of Sin, and That Wicked One.

> "Watch out that you are not deceived. For many will come in my name, claiming I am he, and, the time is near." (Luke 21:8)
>
> And you hear of wars and revolutions, do not be frightened." "Nations will rise against nations, and kingdoms against kingdoms." (Luke 21:9–10)
>
> When he open the second seal, I heard the second creature say, "Come!" And out came another horse, bright red; its rider was permitted to take peace from the earth, so that men should slay one another; and he was given a sword. The sword would be revolution. The red horse, whose rider has a sword, military leader permitted take peace from the earth by creating war and bloodshed. (Revelation 6:3–4)

My America, we have seen some of the results of the rider on the red horse in today's world, the communist government of Red Russia and Red China killing people by the millions. Starting in the year 2014, the terrorists of ISIS , killing people in Iraq and Syria and other countries including are own land. Be aware of the rider on the red horse, wars been around for hundred of years until the end of time. Finally, there will be the final battle—the Battle of Armageddon, the War of all Wars.

The evil of terrorism started with 9/11 in America. Terrorism is now the number one threat against our America and other countries around the world. Our country now has the backing of Homeland Security for our protection, plus our brave and strong military are there for us to provide us with both protection and safety.

The world, including America, has see more crime, violence, and terrorist attacks in malls, military bases, and school campuses. There seems to be no end.

It's one of the signs of the end-times or the last days.

> "and there will be famines."
>
> "and there will be great earthquakes, and in various places famine and pestilences." (Matt. 24:7, Luke 21:11)
>
> When the Lamb opened the third seal, I heard the living creature say, "Come!" I looked, and there before me was a black horse! Its rider was holding a pair of scales in his hand. Then I heard what sounded like a voice among the four living creatures, saying "A quart of wheat for day's wages, and three quarts of barley for a day's wages, and do not damage the oil and the wine!" (Rev. 6:5-6)

A balance or scales indicate commerce, known as capitalism. A denarius was the customary wage of a laborer for one day. One loaf of bread for one day's wages, to feed himself and his family. It will become a time of stealing another man's bread to feed himself and his family to keep themselves from starvation. About 25 percent of the world's children go to bed hungry. This is happening now in the twenty-first century.

This will affect the world economy. Inflation will be on the increase with big demand and supply for food. There will be food shortage, creating more starvation. Will there be people killing each other for food, and will people be eating other humans? Like in the Great Depression of the 1930s, there will be people standing in soup lines for food and water. Only the ones that have the mark of the beast—666—will be able to buy or sell. Without that mark, many people will not have any income or a job. It will be a time of being unable to buy or sell, and in time, it will come to pass.

> When the Lamb opened the fourth seal, I heard the voice of the fourth living creature say, "Come!" I looked, and there was a pale horse! Its rider was named Death, and Hades was following close behind him. They were given power over fourth of the earth to kill by sword, famine and plague, and by the wild beasts of the earth. (Revelation 6:7–8)

Just think of the population of the world, the rider of the pale horse will kill a fourth the people of the earth. Even the animals will attack people. Maybe it's your pet cat or dog; only time will tell what will happen. In our lifetime, we have seen different kinds of virus like HIV, *E. coli*, and now *Ebola* of the twenty-first century striking across the world.

In other words, warfare is followed by inflation and famine. Then hell comes after death.

> I looked up again-and there before me were four chariots coming out from between two mountain-mountains of bronze. The first chariot had red horses, the second black, the third white, and the fourth dappled- all them powerful. These are the four spirits of heaven, going out from standing in the presence of the Lord of the whole earth. The one with the black horses is going toward the north country, the one with white horses toward the west, and the one with dappled horses toward the south." (Zech. 6:1–6)

We are seeing these conditions today in our modern age world—disease, poverty, and primitive living conditions. In some parts of our world, life expectancy is only about forty years old. Yes, the evil Four Horsemen of the Apocalypse are riding their white, red, black, and pale horses galloping across our land yesterday, today, and mostly tomorrow. These four events will indeed devastate the earth. The four horsemen will come riding to bring devastation in the world, on the people who choose wickedness rather than accept the invitation of God.

Whatever you do, don't be involved or be part of these Four Horsemen of Apocalypse. Before Jesus comes for His church, be sure that you are *born again*, or *saved*. Then you will be safe in the living care of the Lord Jesus.

> When he opened the fifth seal, I saw under the altar the souls of those who had been slain because of the word of God and the testimony they had maintained. (Revelation 6:9)
>
> I watched as he opened the sixth seal. There was a great earthquake. The sun turned black like sackcloth made of goat hair, the whole moon turned blood red, and the stars in the sky fell to earth. Every mountain and island was removed from its place. (Revelation 6:12–14)
>
> When he opened the seventh seal, there was silence in heaven for about half an hour. (Revelation 8:1)

22

IN THE OLD Testament times, the trumpet served to announce important events and give signals in time of war. The following seven trumpets is a series of plaques more sever than the seven seals.

The trumpets of history sounded to alert people of another judgment. The trumpet blast was a call for people come back with a relationship with their God.

> Now the seven angels who had the seven trumpets made ready to blow them. The first angel blew his trumpet, and hail and fire, mixed with blood, and it was hurled down upon the earth. So a third of the trees and green grass on earth was burned up. (Revelation 8:6–7)
>
> The second angel blew his trumpet, and something like a huge mountain, all ablaze, was thrown into the sea. A third of the sea turned into blood, a third

of living creatures in the sea died, and a third of the ships were destroyed. (Revelation 8:8–9)

The third angel sounded his trumpet, and a great star, blazing like a torch, fell from the sky on third of the rivers and springs of water—the name of the star is Wormwood. A third of the water turned bitter, and many of the people died from the water that became bitter. (Revelation 8:10–11)

The fourth angel sounded his trumpet, and a third of the sun was struck, a third of the moon, and a third of the stars, so that a third of them turned dark. A third of the day was without light, and also a third of the night. (Revelation 8:12)

"If those days had not been cut short, no one would survive, but for the sake of the elect those days will be shortened." (Matt. 24:22)

The fifth angel sounded his trumpet, and I saw a star had fallen from the sky to the earth. The star was given the key to the shaft of the Abyss. When he opened the Abyss smoke rose from it like a gigantic furnace. The sun and sky were darkened by the smoke from the Abyss. And out the smoke locusts came down upon the earth, and were given power like that of scorpions of the earth. They were told not to harm the grass of the earth or any plant or tree, but only those people who did not have the seal of God on their forehead. They were not given power to kill them, but only to torture them for five

> months. And the agony they suffered was like a sting of a scorpion when it strikes a man. During those days men will seek death, but will not find it; they long to die, but death will elude them. (Rev. 9:1-6)
>
> The sixth angel sounded his trumpet, and I heard a voice from the horns of the golden altar that is before God. It said to the sixth angel who had the trumpet, "Release the four angels who are bound at the great river Euphrates." And the four angels who had been kept ready for this very hour and day and month and year were released to kill a third of mankind. The number of mounted troops was two hundred million. I heard their number. The sixth angel sounded his trumpet, and I heard a voice coming from the horns of the golden altar that is before God. It said to the sixth angel who had the trumpet, "Release the four angels who are bound at the great river Euphrates." To kill third of mankind. (Rev. 9:13–15)

The fall season of 2011, there was an estimated 7 billion people in the world, one third of that total number be over 2.3 billion people.

> Then I saw another mighty angel coming down from heaven. But in the days when the seven angel is about to sound his trumpet, the mystery of God will be accomplished, just as he announced to his servants the prophets. Then the voice that I heard

> from heaven spoke to me once more. "Go, take the scroll that lies open in the hand of the angel who standing on the sea and on the land." So I went to the angel and asked him to give me the litle scroll. He said to me, "Take it and eat it. It will turn your stomach sour, but in your mouth as sweet as honey." I took the little scroll from the angel's hand and ate it. It tasted as sweet as honey in my mouth, but when I had eaten it, my stomach turned sour. Then I was told, "You must prophesy again about many peoples, nations, languages and kings." (Rev. 10: 1, 7-11)

Because of that old supply-and-demand system, people will be standing in lines for food, gas, medical needs, water, and other various needs.

> Dear children, this is the last hour, and you heard that the Antichrist is coming. Even now, many Antichrists have come. This is how we know it is the last hour. (1 John 2:18)

> "The sun will be darkened, and the moon will not give light; the stars will fall from the sky, and the heavenly bodies will be shaken." (Matt. 24:29)

> God's message is His intention of the sounding of the seven trumpets by the seven angels is not to inflict vengeance but bring repentance.

23

According to Daniel's 70 Weeks, the weeks will last for seven years. The hardest and worst part will be the last three and a half years known as the Great Tribulation. We have the same reading from the book of Revelation—that the Great Tribulation will last three and one-half years. It will be time and times and half, same as 42 months or three and a half years. The Great Tribulation will be the worst of times the unsaved people on the earth will have to face.

> He shall speak against the Most High, and oppress his saints and try to change the set times and the laws. The saints be handed over to him for time and times and half a time. Daniel 7:25
>
> Then I heard a loud voice from the temple saying to the seven angels, "Go and pour out the seven bowls of God's wrath on the earth." (Revelation 16:1)

This will take place during the Great Tribulation period, the last three and half years, as things become worst under the power of the Antichrist. According to the Bible, the Bowl Judgment consisting of the following:

> The first angel went and poured his bowl on the land, and ugly painful sores broke out on the people who had the mark of the beast and who worshiped his image. (Revelation 16:2)

> The second angel poured out his bowl into the sea, and it turned into blood like that of a dead man, and every living thing in the sea died. (Revelation 16:3)

> The third angel poured out his bowl on the rivers and springs of water, and they become blood. (Revelation 16:4)

> The fourth angel poured out his bowl on the sun, and the sun was given power to scorch people with fire. They were seared by the intense heat and cursed the name of God, who had control over these plagues, but they refused to repent and glorify him. (Revelation 16:8–9)

> The fifth angel poured out his bowl on the throne of the beast, and his kingdom was plunged into darkness. Men gnawed their tongues in agony and cursed the God of heaven because of the pains and their sores, but they refused to repent of what they had done. (Revelation 16:10–11)

The sixth angel poured his bowl on the great river Euphrates, and its water dried up to prepare the way for the kings from the East. Then I saw three evil spirits that looked like frogs, they came out of the mouth of the dragon, out the mouth of the beast and out of the mouth of the false prophet. They are spirits of the demons performing miraculous signs, and they go out to the kings of the whole world, to gather them for the battle on the great day of God Almighty. Then they gathered the kings together to the place called, Armageddon. (Revelation 16:12–14, 16)

The seventh angel poured out his bowl into the air, and out of the temple came a loud voice came from the throne, saying, "It is done." Then there came flashes of lighting, rumbling, pearls of thunder and a severe earthquake. No earthquake like it has ever occurred since man has been on earth, so tremendous was the quake. The great city split into three parts, and the cities of the nations collapsed. God remembered Babylon the Great and gave her the cup filled with the wine of the fury of his wrath. Every island fled away and the mountains could not be found. From the sky huge hail stones of about a hundred pounds each fell upon men. And they cursed God on account of the plague of hail, because the plague was so terrible. (Revelation 16:17–21)

Immediately after the distress of those days. The sun will be darkened, and the moon will not give its light: the stars will fall from the sky. And the heavenly bodies will be shaken. (Matt.24:29)

24

Like the days of Moses in Egypt—"Let my people go"— many people of the Great Tribulation will go thru the three Judgments will kept on blasphemed God in heaven and still will not want to repent. Sounds like the old saying "What goes around comes around," this time its not because of mankind but from God's words and His works of the wrath to come. It seems over the thousands of years, mankind has not learned the ways of God's ways or the words of His Ten Commandments; that people would change from their sinful ways.

The three evil ones will be running here and there destroying the earth and its people. These evil ones are Satan the devil, the Antichrist, and the False Prophet. Beware of these three evil ones. Satan the devil is alive today in our world. The other two will be coming after the Rapture of His church. Come, Lord Jesus, the believers are watching and waiting so that you may take us believers to our heavenly home.

> And war broke out in heaven; Michael and his angels fought against the dragon and his angels, but they did not prevail, nor was a place found for them in heaven any longer. So the dragon who is called Satan the devil, who deceives the whole world with his angels were cast out to the earth. (Revelation 12:7, 9)

Since that time so many years ago, Satan the devil has been deceiving people here in America and in other countries around the world. This Evil One doesn't give up. He was there trying to deceive Jesus in his time, and now he is deceiving us Christians today and the days and years yet to come.

> And I saw a beast rising up out of the sea, the dragon gave the beast his power, his throne, and great authority. The whole world was astonished, worshiped, and followed the beast. The beast was given a mouth to utter proud words and blasphemies, and to exercise his authority for forty-two months. He opened his mouth to blaspheme God, and to slander his name and his dwelling places and those who lives in heaven. He was given power to make war against the saints and to conquer them. And he was given authority over every tribe, people, language and nations. All inhabitants of the earth will worship the beast—all whose names have not been written in the book of life belonging to the Lamb. (Revelation 13:1–3, 5–9)

Dear children, this is the last hour, and as you have heard, the Antichrist is coming. Even now, many Antichrists have come and deceived us. This we know, for it is the last hour.

The book of Revelation relates that the Antichrist will be able to track and control all financial transactions and no man will be able to buy or sell anything unless he has the mark 666 on the right hand or the forehead. John says that it is a human number—that is, it's the number of a person name.

He forced everyone—small and great, rich or poor, free and slave—to receive a mark on his right hand or on his forehead, so that no one could buy or sell unless he had the mark, which is the name of the beast or the number of his name.

At one time in the past years, this was not possible now with microchips, modern computer technology, MRI testing, and smart cards, people can be traced anywhere in the world. Where you do your banking or shopping, there are cameras watching you. Yes, Big Brother is there watching you all the time. With a microchip inserted in your right hand or forehead showing all your records, there is no way you will be buying or selling without the mark of the beast. Without the mark of 666, there will be no jobs for those faithful people. The Bible says in the end-times or last days of this church age, knowledge shall increase. That time is *now*. These will be trying times. People will have nowhere to turn to for help about what to do with their family and their own lives. People refusing the mark of 666 will beheaded. We are seeing something like that in our twenty-first century: the ISIS terrorists are beheading Christians in various countries. During the times of the Great Tribulation, the beheading of Christians will be worse than that by ISIS.

> Then I saw another beast, coming up out of the earth. He had two horns like a lamb, but he spoke like a dragon. He exercised all the authority of the first beast on his behalf, and made the earth and its inhabitants worship the first beast, whose fatal wound had been healed. He performed great and miraculous signs, even cause fire come down from heaven to earth in full view of men. Because of the signs he was given power to do on behalf of the first beast, he deceived the inhabitants of the earth. He was given power to give breath to the image of the first beast, so that it could speak and cause all who refused to worship the image to be killed. He also forced everyone, small and great, rich and poor, free and slave, to received a mark on his right hand or on his forehead. So that no one could buy or sell unless he had the mark, which is the name of the beast or the number of his name. (Revelation 13:11–17)

The second beast following the first beast, the Antichrist, will lead the unsaved people of the entire world to worship the Antichrist. Bible scholars have called the second beast the False Prophet. He will be a counterfeit Christian leader. Some Bible preachers and teachers are saying it might be the last Pope, known as the evil Pope?

The Antichrist and the False Prophet are the two leaders of the Great Tribulation. The Antichrist will be the political leader and the False Prophet will be the spiritual leader. During the Great Tribulation time, people that accepted the New World Order must and will worship the Antichrist.

> "How long will it be before these astonishing things are fulfilled."
>
> "It will be for a time, times, and half a time. When the power of the holy people has been finally broken, all these things will be completed. Many will be purified, made spotless and refine, and the wicked will continued be wicked. None of the wicked will understand, but those who are wise will understand." (Dan. 12:6–7, 12:10)

Just as there is a Holy Trinity of God the Father, Jesus Christ the Son, and the Holy Spirit, so we will find that Satan has devised his own trinity for the end-times. Together with Satan as the unholy God, the Antichrist as the unholy son, the False Prophet is the third party of the unholy trinity.

> God is just. He will pay back trouble to those who trouble you and give relief to you who are troubled,

and to us as well. This will happen when the Lord Jesus is revealed from heaven in blazing fire with his powerful angels. He will punish those who do not know God and do not obey the gospel of our Lord Jesus. They will be punished with everlasting destruction and shut out from the presence of the Lord and from the majesty of his power on the day he comes to be glorified in his holy people and to be marveled at among all those who have believed. This includes you, because you believed our testimony to you. (2 Thess. 1:6–10)

Concerning the coming of our Lord Jesus Christ and our being gathered to him, we ask you brothers, but to become easily unsettled or alarmed by some prophecy, report or letter supported to have come from us, saying that the day of the Lord has already come. Don't let anyone deceived you in any way, for that day will not come until the rebellion occurs and the man of lawlessness is revealed, the man doomed to destruction. He will oppose and exalt himself over everything that is called God or is worshiped, so that he sets himself up in God's temple, proclaiming himself to be God. (2 Thess. 2:1–4)

These will be hard, horror, and sad times for the unsaved people. Their hearts will be hardened and not want to change. They will keep on cussing and denigrating our God with hate in their hearts and minds. Like the people of Moses's times, they will never change. Will the people of our world ever change or learn from their sinful ways?

Like the kings of the Old Testaments, there were some good kings, and God bless them and God bless the Holy Land because of these good kings. Also, some kings that were not good, God turned his back on that king and the land of Israel. This is true with the politician leaders of our America, more so in the last sixty-plus years. The situation has gone from bad to worse in this new twenty-first century. Since the national elections of 2008 and 2012, God has not been in our America because of our greedy and unfaithful leaders. Our political leaders are more concerned with their own jobs in the next election than they are with unknown financial conditions that are facing our America. The last few midterms or national elections, the president and members of Congress were more concerned with staying in office for another four years. Is this right for America when we are facing hard financial times, as people are losing their homes and jobs? The taxpayers and voters of America, it's in your hands. Be sure to vote in the next election. Let's make your vote count and your voice heard as you will be expressing your opinion. The buck stops with you, not with the president. Just remember, the federal government works for you, and don't forget it.

We need more business-minded, faithful, strong leadership in our nation—both in the business world and in our local, state, and federal governments. Only

God-believing and God-fearing leadership people in both business and federal government are needed for taking our America forward as a stronger financial and greater military world power nation. These God-believing and God-fearing leaders must be sowing seeds of faith for a greater and stronger nation. Have the people of this America forgotten God and made the federal government their God? Has our God turned his back on America in the last sixty-some years? Is this why our nation is so messed up and our government leaders are confused and can't make sound decisions? Prayers by believing people, and God will hear those prayers. There is still time to turn this country around. Otherwise, we will be seeing our America blowing in the wind.

> In the last days, God says, I will pour out my Spirit on all people. Your sons and daughters will prophesy, your young men will see visions, your old men will dream dreams. Even on my servants, both men and women, I will pour out my Spirit in those days, and they will prophesy. I will show wonders in heaven above and signs on earth below, blood and fire and billows of smoke. The sun will be turned to darkness and the moon to blood before the coming of the great and glorious day of the Lord. And everyone who calls on the name of the Lord will be saved. (Acts 2:17–21)

25

THE CHURCH WILL be caught up in the Rapture before the seven-year tribulation, but God is going to reach out to the lost people during the Tribulation. Those left behind after the Rapture can be saved, but it will be difficult.

> After this I looked and there before me a great multitude that no man could count, from every nations, tribe, people and language, standing before the throne and in front of the Lamb. They were wearing white robes and were holding palms branches in their hands. And they cried with a loud voice. Salvation belongs to our God, who sits on the throne, and to the Lamb. (Revelation 7:9–10)

God has a salvation plan for the people that did not take the mark of the beast, for God has a way and they are as follows:

The Two Witnesses, the 144,000 Jewish Witnesses, the Angel of Everlasting Gospel, and the major outpouring of the Holy Spirit. These are the ones that will bring salvation to the unsaved people during those troubled times—that is, if the unsaved want to change.

> The Two Witnesses will serve from Jerusalem as God's mighty witnesses, and they will boldly preach God's truth and perform awesome miracles. The two Witnesses walking with the full power of God will come forth prophesying on God's behave to the whole world for 1,260 days, clothed in sackcloth. They are the two olive trees, and the two candlesticks standing before the God of the earth. If anyone tries to harm them, fire comes from their mouths and devours their enemies. These men have power to shut up the sky so that it will not rain during the time they are prophesying; and they have power to turn waters into blood and to strike the earth with every kind of plague as often as they want.
>
> When the Two Witnesses have finished their testimony, the beast will come up from the Abyss will attack them and overpower and kill them. Their bodies will lie in the street of the great city, which is where our Lord was crucified. For three and a half days, men from every people, tribe, language, and nation will glaze on their bodies and refuse them burial (Rev. 11:3-9).

> After three and a half days a breath of life from God entered the Two Witnesses, and they stood up on their feet, and terror struck those who saw them. Then they heard a loud voice from heaven saying "Come up here." And they went up to heaven in a cloud, while their enemies looked up.
> (Revelation 11:11–12)

They will be seen worldwide through satellite TV, for the evil people to see. God is always in control, as the two Witnesses will be going home to heaven and be with their Lord Jesus. The new saved people will have an ear to hear and an eye to see, but it is God that has His eyes on them by means of the Two Witnesses. Blessed are those ones that are saved during the Tribulation's time of trouble—they will be living in the New Heaven and the New Jerusalem with the rest of us believers.

Some Christian scholars have argued over who are the Two Witnesses, that they might be Elijah and Moses. Some Bible preachers believe they are Elijah and Enoch. These are the ones that had the power from God to perform miracles and be prophets. Now is the time during this church age to reach out to the unsaved so that they will not have to go through the time of trouble. Elijah the man of God was taken up to heaven in a whirlwind in a chariot of fire . Enoch walked with God 300 years. Then he was no more, and God took him away to his presence without him experiencing death.

> Then I looked, and there before me was the Lamb, standing on Mount Zion, and with him 144,000 who had his name and his Father's name written on their foreheads. These are those who did not defile themselves with women, for they kept themselves pure. They follow the Lamb wherever he goes. No lie was found in their mouths, they are blameless. (Revelation 14:1, 4–5)

The 144,000 are a special group of people who completely surrendered to the Lord and followed Jesus in all His ways. They are the 12,000 each from the twelve tribes of Israel who committed their lives 100 percent to the Lord. These are the twelve tribes of Israel:

Judah, Reuben, Gad, Asher, Naphtali, Manasseh, Simeon, Levi, Issachar, Zebulun, Joseph, and Benjamin. They have the Seal of God, which symbolizes that they belong to God as his spiritual children. These 144,000 will have the faith in Jesus as their Savior in this later-day revival of the nation of Israel. God will protect these special people during the wrath for they have the mark of God.

The angels will judge the earth during the seven-year tribulation. These are three Everlasting Angels during this seven-year time, and they each have a purpose. These angels fly in the heaven midst an having the every lasting Gospel. These angels will fly in the heaven with the power of the everlasting gospel of our Lord Jesus (Revelation 17:5).

- The first Everlasting Angel has a message to prepare the world for the Second Coming of Jesus Christ.
- The second Everlasting Angel has a message of calling for repentance.
- The third Everlasting Angel has a warning to the people of the earth not to worship the beast or his image.

The Holy Spirit will still be very active on earth, convicting people of their sins and drawing them near to the Lord.

The Bible has given us signs that we are living in the end-times, or last days, of His church age. Our Lord said, "When you see these things that I have told you begin to come to pass, then look up for your redemption draweth nigh." The coming of our Lord Jesus Christ is the backbone and the heartbeat that is written in the book of Revelation. My dear brothers and sisters in Christ, our Lord Jesus said keep looking up.

The blessed hope of the church is the return of Christ to take His church home before the rapture. The blessed hope of Israel is the second coming of her Messiah, the Lord Jesus Christ. The hope of the world is the coming of our Lord, and he will do this in Glory. Before the Rapture of His church, always be ready and watch for His coming in the clouds. That time is more apparent now than any other time in our lives. Just look around and you'll see what has happened in our world. Always "keep looking up" for His Coming will be very soon in the clouds.

> For the grace of God that brings salvation has appeared to all men. It teaches us to say "No" to ungodliness and worldly passions, and to live self controlled, upright and godly lives in this present age, while we wait for the blessed hope-the glorious appearing of our great God and Savior, Jesus Christ, who give himself for us to redeem us from wickedness and to purity for himself a people that are his very own, eager to do what is good. These, then, are the things you should teach. Encourage and rebuke with all authority. Do not let anyone despise you. (Tit. 2:11–15)

26

FOR ALMOST TWO thousand years, Babylon, during the years of King Nebuchadezzar, was the most important city in the world. Because of its center location, it became a great commercial and financial center for its time. Over the years, this city changed kings, and it became the capital of the Persian Empire. Next, the Greeks conquered the Persians about the year 331 BC, and Alexander the Great made Babylon his capital. After many centuries, this great city has been dead in the dust for ages.

Yes, this old city will come back alive, for it is in the process of being rebuilt during the late twentieth century and into the new twenty-first century. When President Saddam Hussein rose in power in Iraq, he wanted to be like that King Nebuchadezzar. Hussein started rebuilding this modern city again, which is near his capital city of Baghdad. Most of the money to rebuild this city of

Babylon has come from the export of black gold, which Iraq is very rich in. There will always be richness for Iraq, for the whole world needs and wants oil. Otherwise, the whole world of commerce would quit going around. Even, the United Nations is pumping plenty of money in this rebuilding project. The United States government is taking steps in the rise of this city and that of Iraq for the future of the world.

It will become the world capital for banking and of various corporations, plus those of shipping, as they set up this city for their center for business. Babylon will be the world's playground for gambling and all kinds of pleasures. It will be a time like that of "Happy days are here again" for this great business-minded city. In time, Babylon will become a city full of sin and vice. The Antichrist will take control of the world for his government. There will be three key cities under his command. From Babylon, the Antichrist will set up his economic and financial empire. From the city of Jerusalem, he will be in control of religion; and from the city of Rome, the beast will rule the political world. During this time, the unsaved people of Babylon will turn their backs on God and turn to material things.

For God will hear from heaven all the sins and vices of Babylon. Next, God will pour out His judgment upon this city of Babylon.

And on her forehead a name is written:

MYSTERY, BABYLON THE GREAT, THE MOTHER OF HARLOTS AND THE ABOMINATIONS OF THE EARTH.

After this I saw another Angel coming down from heaven. He had great authority, and the earth was illuminated by his splendor. With a mighty voice, he shouted:

Fallen! Fallen is Babylon the Great! (Rev. 18:1–2)

For all the nations have drunk the maddening wine of her adulteries. The kings of the earth committed adultery with her, and the merchants of the earth grew rich from excessive luxuries. Then I heard from heaven say:

She will be consumed by fire, for mighty is the Lord God who judges her. When the kings of the earth who committed adultery with her and share her luxury, they will weep and mourn over her. The merchants of the earth will weep and mourn over her because no one buys their cargo any more. Every sea captain, and all who travel by ship, the sailors, and all who earn their living from the sea, will stand far off. When they see the smoke of her burning, they will exclaim., "Was there ever a city like this great city?"

WOE! WOE! O GREAT CITY." (Rev. 18:3-10)

After this I heard what sounded like the roar of a great multitude in heaven shoulting:

Hallelujah! Salvation and glory and power belong to our God." (Revelation 19:1)

Babylon the city that Was so Great centuries ago, become the city that Is so Great during the time of the Great Tribulation, and after Christ was done with this city, the city of Babylon went back to its old ways again. Like that old saying "What goes around, comes around" became true again for Babylon.

27

We saw the Four Horsemen of the Apocalypse, Satan the devil, the Antichrist, and the False Prophet spreading horror across the world. Now there is another horseman coming—it's the fifth Horseman of the Apocalypse. It's the Second Coming of our Lord Jesus Christ, for He is coming in power and great glory.

> At that time, the sign of the Son of Man will appear in the sky, and all the nations of the earth will mourn. They will see the Son of Man coming on the cloud of the sky, with power and great glory. And he will send his angels with a loud trumpet call, and they will gather his elect from the four winds, from one end of the heavens to the other. (Matt. 24:30–31)
>
> I saw heaven standing open, and there before me was a white horse whose rider is called Faithful and True. With justice he judges and makes war. His

> eyes are like blazing fire, and on his head are many crowns. He has a name written on him that no one knows but he himself. He is dressed in a robe dipped in blood, and his name is called The Word of God. The armies of heaven, were following him, riding on white horses and dress in fine linen, white and clean. (Revelation 19:11–14)
>
> "See, the Lord cometh with ten thousands of his saints" (Jude 1:14)

For John saw Heaven open up, the one riding the white horse is Jesus Christ. The Fifth Horseman of the Apocalypse riding out of Heaven and he will be riding in wonderful glory and with great power. Throughout the ages there was talk, that Jesus was gentle, meek, and mild. Now he is coming to judge the world with a sword out of his mouth. This sword is The Word of God.

This will be an exciting time for the ten thousand saints that will be riding in battle on white horses with our Lord. Yes, we that are born again or saved will be part of God's heavenly army going to battle with our Holy Lord Jesus. Christ will come with a vast army of saints, who are the born again people. We will fight by His side as He puts down the evil ones of the earth. Then we will sit upon thrones of judgment with Him, and we shall judge the world.

> Now out of His mouth comes a sharp sword, with which strike down the nations. He will rule them

with an iron scepter. He treads the winepress of the fury of the wrath God Almighty. On his robe and on his thigh has his name written:

KING OF KINGS AND LORD OF LORDS (Revelation 19:15–16)

The Lord Jesus with his heavenly armies will be facing the enemy of the North (Russia), the enemy of the South (the Middle East countries), the East known (China), and lastly, the enemy of the West (Europe and what is left of North and South America). In those last days, China will become a great and powerful financial and military country. We are now seeing China in this twenty-first century, becoming a more financially powerful and strong country, and they easily could have an army of 200 million strong.

> Then I saw the beast and the kings of the earth and their armies gathered together to make war against the rider on the horse and his army. (Revelation 19:19)
>
> I saw an angel standing in the sun, who cried in a loud voice to all the birds that fly in midst, "Come," gather together for the great supper of God, so that you may eat the flesh of kings, generals, and mighty men, of horses and their riders, and the flesh of all people, free and slave, both small and great. (Revelation 19:17–18)

This is called the Battle of Armageddon. The results of this great battle is that the blood of the dead will come up to horses' bridle. It takes place in the northern part of Israel all the way to the southern part known as the Valley of Jehosphaphat, an area approximately two hundred miles. Most of the famous battles of Israel have occurred in the plain of Megiddo. This valley has seen many battles and wars over thousands of years. Now it's the final battle; it will be the War of all Wars.

> But the beast was captured, and with him the false prophet, these two were cast alive into the lake of fire burning sulfur. And I saw an angel coming down out of from heaven, having the key to the Abyss and holding in his hand a great chain. He sized the dragon, who is the devil, or Satan, and bound him for a thousand years. Threw him into the Abyss and lock and seal keeping him from deceiving the nations anymore until the thousand years are over. After that, he must be set free for a short time. (Revelation 19:20, 20:1–3)

> Then I saw a great white throne and him who was seated on it. And I saw the dead, great and small, standing before the throne, and books were opened. Another book was opened which is the book of life. The dead was judged according to what they had done as is recorded in the books. If anyone's name was not founded in the book of life, he was thrown into the lake of fire. (Rev. 20:11–12, 15)

28

ACCORDING TO THE Bible, the Millennium is the one thousand year rule of Jesus Christ on the earth, which will occur right after the Great Tribulation.

> The nation in the world will beat their swords into plowshares, and their spears into pruning hooks. Nations shall not take up sword against nations, nor will they train for war anymore. (Isa. 2:4)
>
> The wolf will live the lamb, the leopard will lie down with the goat, the calf and the lion and the yearling together; and a child will lead them. They will neither harm nor destroy on all my holy mountain, for the earth will be full of the knowledge of the Lord as the waters cover the sea. (Isa. 11:6, 11:9)
>
> I saw thrones on which were seated those who had been given authority to judge. And I saw the souls of those who had been beheaded because of their

> testimony for Jesus and because of the word of God. They had not worship the beast or his image and had not received the mark on their foreheads or on their hands. They came to life and reigned with Christ for a thousand years. (Revelation 20:4)

The millennium is a long time. People during those years will still have children, and in turn, their children will have children. There will still be sin during that time. Those children may not have the same kind of faith as their parents. It will be a different kind of sin during this millennium time. It will not be temptation of Satan. This kind of sin during this time period will be one's own human nature. Of course, the Evil One will take advantage of these kinds of unfaithful sinners. Ole Satan will be released from the bottomless pit to deceive for the last time. But God has other plans for all of them—it will be fire coming down from heaven and devouring them.

When the thousand years are over, Satan will be released from his prison and will go out to deceive the nations in the four corners of the earth—Gog and Magog—to gather them for battle. In number, they are like the sand on the seashore. They marched across the breadth of the earth and surrounded the camp of God's people, the city he loves. But fire came down from heaven and devoured them. And the devil who deceived them was thrown into the lake of burning sulfur, where the beast and the false prophet had been thrown. They will be tormented day and night forever and ever.

29

There is coming a day when the kingdoms of this world will become the kingdom of our Christ, for He is the King of kings and the Lord of lords. We are the ones that are born again, the saved ones; and we will reign with Him forever and ever.

After the events of the end-times, the current heaven and earth will pass away and be replaced by the new heaven and new earth. It's on the new earth where the New Jerusalem, the heavenly city, will be located. The new earth will be free from death, evil, sickness, sin, and suffering. It will be a place where we will dwell with glorified physical bodies. All God's children will live in a new, sin-free physical bodies. That is, our bodies will be like Christ's resurrected body, and they will be glorious, imperishable, and powerful. Thank you, Lord Jesus, that that you have given us, your children, the perfect body that will be just like yours.

"Behold, I will create new heaven and a new earth. The former things will not be remembered, nor will they come to mind. But be glad and rejoice forever in what I will create, for I will create Jerusalem to be a delight and people to joy. I will rejoice over Jerusalem and take a delight and its people a joy. I will rejoice over Jerusalem and take delight in my people; the sound of weeping and crying will be heard in it no more." (Isa. 65:17–19)

But in keeping with his promise we are looking to a new heaven and a new Earth, the home of rightness. (2 Pet. 3:13)

Then I saw a new heaven and a new earth for the first heaven and the first earth had passed away. I saw the Holy City, the new Jerusalem, coming down out of heaven from God, prepared as a bride beautifully dressed prepared for her husband. And I heard a loud voice from the throne saying. Now the dwelling of God is with men, and he will live with them. They will be his people, and God himself will be with them and be their God. He will wipe every tear from their eyes. There will be no more death, or mourning or crying or pain, for the old order of things has passed away. The New Jerusalem is the church, which is the light of the world. (Revelation 21:1–4)

"Behold, I am coming soon! Blessed is he who keeps the words of the prophecy in this book." (Revelation 22:7)

> "I, Jesus, have sent my angel to give you this testimony for the churches. I am the Root and the Offspring of David, and the bright Morning Star." (Revelation 22:16)

The Bible opens and closes with basically the same type of setting. Two chapters of Genesis is God's creation of heaven and earth and preparing for mankind. The last part of the Bible is the book of Revelation, that our God is creating the New World, New Heaven, and that of the New Jerusalem, all coming down from heaven for all the born again or saved people living with their Lord.

He will come in the fullness of His glory to execute His wrath on those who rejected Him and to receive into His glory those who believe in Him. The believers in their glorified bodies will be like our Lord Jesus in His glorified body. The people will be free to come and go into the new city of Jerusalem. This new city will be our temple. All the believers that are saved will be there near our Lord Jesus. What a glorious time that will be—a time of living with Jesus forever and ever with no end. Yes, most important of all is we will see Him face-to-face. We will be singing and shouting in victory.

> How great is the love the Father has lavished on us, that we should be called children of God. And that is what we are! But we know that when Christ appears, we shall be like him, for we shall see him as he is. Everyone who have this hope in him purify himself, just as he is pure. [1 John 3:1–3]

We are living in this old world as a temporary home. Yes, we are almost home. Being believers in our Lord Jesus, we will be living in the New Earth and seeing the new city of Jerusalem.

The purpose of Jesus's First Coming was to have a plan of salvation for us, that is, being born again or being saved. That plan was carried out on the cross in Calvary. Being born again or being saved is the process of going through three steps of repentance, then baptism, and then that of the resurrection. Being born again is getting your name in the Lamb's Book of Life. Amen and amen. When a person dies, their spirit goes directly to heaven or to hell. The answer for your salvation is only believed that Jesus is your Lord and Savior. The good news is that Jesus Christ is our King of kings and the Lord of lords. He is Alive yesterday, today, and tomorrow for you and your family. Just believe.

> Therefore, if anyone is in Christ, he is a new creation; the old has gone, the new has come! What a great promise because it came from God. (2 Corinthians 5:17–18)

30

THESE ARE THE conditions of society as history teaches:

- Bondage to spiritual faith
- Spiritual faith to great courage
- Great courage to liberty
- Liberty to abundance and selfishness
- Abundance and selfishness to apathy
- Apathy to decay
- Decay to dependence
- Dependence back to bondage

The year 2015 and the years of the future, what should the people of America be doing during these end-times, or last days? Americans of the new twenty-first century, let's stand firm and tall as Christians—with dreams, hopes, and visions like that of our Founding Fathers of 1776. Also, keep on believing in those famous words of both President John F. Kennedy and Dr. Martin King Jr.: "Ask not what your country can do for you, ask what you can do for your country." And "I have a dream."

America, let's put our hands to the plow and sow seeds of faith for a better and greater nation. Plow deep and wide that those faith seeds will have deeper roots, that our nation can go forward being financially and militarily strong again. My Americans, don't let your dreams and hopes be blowing in the wind. Let's stand firm and tall for our America today and all the tomorrows to come. Do it for your children and their children.

31

I WANT BRING up the subject of December 21, 2012, since it's been on the minds of many people during those times of the twenty-first century. This date December 21, 2012, we had been reading articles in books, newspapers, or seeing various reports on the History TV channel, and now there is a Hollywood movie on the subject.

Recalling the year 1999, when people of the world had fears as the calendar was shifting into the new century with the year 2000. It was the Y2K panic. People were stocking up on food supplies and preparing for the worldwide collapse. The final result was that there was very little change that took place after that so-called dreadful date. Will this be the same story on and after that date of December 21, 2012. Only time will tell, and it did. No change.

It's about what was going to happen to our world on December 21, 2012. It's mostly based upon the Maya people, the ancient times of southern Mexico and Central America known for their advanced understanding of astronomy. The Mayan 5125-year-old calendar uses astrology rather than faith regarding the last days on earth. They were well ahead of their time regarding tracking the solar system. They believed that the sun would line up to the Milky Way. On that day there would be catastrophic earthquakes, the earth burned by solar flares, worldwide floods, and reversal of the North and South Poles.

We were hearing similar reports by the Hopi Indians of Southwestern United States. They were telling about warnings of major structure of the earth and the climate. These Hopi Indians believed that the world will go through four periods: that of volcanoes destroying large animals, the ice age thousands years ago, the flood of Noel's time, and that of the present. These Hopi Indians were seeing major changes that our America and the world will be facing on December 21, 2012.

Likewise, the predictions or visions from Nostradamus (born during the sixteenth century in South France). Many of his prophecies dealt with disasters such as earthquakes, floods, plagues, wars, and the coming three Antichrists—plus, some predictions into the twenty-first century regarding the end-times of the year 2012. Seems strange, that we were getting these three predications of future events in our lifetime, on the same day December 21, 2012. But the doomsday of December 21, 2012, had arrived and gone. The world is still the same as the days, months, and years before.

What does the Word of God tell us about the end-times or the last days? Let's take a look at His words.

> While He was sitting on the Mount of Olives, the disciples approached Him privately And said, "Tell us, when will things happen? And what is the sign of Your coming and the end of the age." Then Jesus replied to them: "watch out that no one deceives you." (Matt. 24:3–4)
>
> "Therefore keep watch, because you don't know the day or the hour." (Matt. 25:13)

Are these the answers to the date of December 21, 2012, or another date of the past or the future? We have heard or seen other predictions of the so-called doomsday, and we will see more in the future from some other person or date. Only God has the real answer regarding the dates and times for the end-times or last days of His church age. Just keep on believing the word from our God, for He holds the whole world in his hand.

32

OUR AMERICA HAS come a long way in the last four hundred years. Starting with the Pilgrims of the 1600s coming across the Atlantic to the New World for freedom of religion and the forming of the thirteen colonies. The 1700s with our faithful Founding Fathers writing and signing our Constitution and the Declaration of Independence of 1776. The 1800s with the freedom from slavery, the Westward movement of the pioneers going across the plains into the Rockies and onto the West Coast of America, and the farmers and ranchers of the Heartland sowing seeds for the bread basket for the hungry and starving world. Those early setters want to know what is beyond those hills, the mountains, and the next valleys as they headed into the Heartland of America. The 1900s with the great industrial movement for the future of America. These are the true and faithful people that were sowing faith seeds for America's roots and at same time sowing seeds for their own family tree roots.

During this new young twenty-first century, is this the time for our Lord Jesus to be coming in the clouds for His church? All the signs have been fulfilled for the Rapture of His church; that time for His coming is very near. God's big clock in heaven is ticking away as we are approaching the high noon hour here in America, or the midnight hour somewhere else in the world. Let's be working for our Lord Jesus up to the time that our Lord will be taking all of us believers up in the big sky to be with Him in heaven. Come soon, Lord Jesus. All the believers are ready, watching, and waiting for your coming. Yes, we are ready.

"Yes, I am coming soon." Amen. Come, Lord Jesus (Rev. 22:20).

We have seen many wars over the years, as well as major financial ups and downs; but the people of America would always roll up their sleeves, got their hands dirty, and they went to work so that your children and grand children will have a greater America. They want a greater country for the next generation, a nation that is one in Victory and a true Winner. It take faith and lots of hard work to make all this come true. America has been real bless in the past years, for we had a strong Christian beginning. We were founded as a Christian nation, we must keep those dreams, hopes, and visions alive in Jesus name.

That old saying "What goes around comes around" is as true today in the twenty-first century as it was in the old days of the Bible. Like Israel in the days of the judges, there were bad and good kings. When you turn your back on God, He will turn his back on America, Israel, or any country of this world. Like in old Israel in the times of judges, our USA has forgotten our heritage and now has forgotten our God. When a country removes prayer and the Ten Commandments in public places, legalizes abortion, and approves same sex marriage in America, our God will turn away from such a country. We are seeing today in America decaying morals, bad business and government ethics, and now a bankrupt and broken country with poor leadership. Like in the days of the old Bible days, Israelites forgot God and chase after other gods. Has our America forgotten God who blesses, heals, and makes this nation so great for so many years? We must be better informed, get involved, and that God will inspired us. The Forty-Fourth President of the USA has turned his back on Israel many times. Be aware, my America, of what is to happen. God will Curse nations that Curse His Holy Land and its people. Has this happened to our America, that God is cursing and turn His back on this country?

All this must change *now*. We must become a faithful and thankful country again. We must elect business-minded, godly leaders in the local, state, and federal governments. It is our duty and honor as Christians to place godly people in the leadership of our nation. Just remember the next time you go to the local, state or national election, vote for the person, not the party. It seems like the people today are always voting for the party, whoever is running for office. We need bigger changes for 2016 and the years to come, such as the following:

- Putting the emergency brakes on federal spending, which has been out of control for years.
- Our federal budget is broken down.
- Improve our tax code, which is overdue.
- Get rid of business red tape and regulations.
- Make improvements in the Medicaid, Medicare, and Social Security programs.
- Sound homeland security and a stronger military.
- Provide better, secure jobs in America.

It's been several years since our big federal government had a good, sound budget. Without good local, state, and federal government budgets, you will be getting runaway spending. This is why we have a bankrupt nation over $19 trillion national debt plus interest going into year 2016.

33

Here are words of wisdoms of years past from Will Rogers and various presidents that is true for today and the years to come:

> There is trick to be humorist when you have the whole government working for you.
> I'm not nearly so concerned about the return on my capital as I am the return of capital.
>
> —Will Rogers

> Educate and inform the whole mass of the people. They are the only sure reliance for the preservation of our liberty.
>
> —President Thomas Jefferson

America is not anything if it consists of each of us. It will is something only if it consist all of us.

—President Woodrow Wilson

Let us have the courage to stop borrowing to meet the continuing deficits. Stop the deficits.

—President Franklin D. Roosevelt"

I was in search of a one-armed economist so that the guy could never make a statement and then say: "on the other hand.

—President Harry S. Truman

Politics ought to be part-time profession of every citizen who would protect the rights and privileges of free people and who preserve what is good and fruitful in our national heritage.

—President Dwight D. Eisenhower

Let every nation know, whether it wishes us well or ill, that we shall pay any price, bear any burden, meet any hardship, support any friend, oppose any foe to assure the survival and success of liberty.

—President John F. Kennedy

If we ever forget that we are One Nation Under God that we will be nation gone under.

—President Ronald Reagan

> We are a nation of communities, a brilliant
> diversity spread like stars, like a thousand points of
> light in a broad and peaceful sky.
>
> —President George H. W. Bush

Let us as believing Christians start praying, that our God will forgive our sins and heal our land again. Our America needs a mighty revival across our nation for a better and greater America. We want a nation that has victory in Jesus, a nation full of the Holy Spirit for a faithful America. Just believe and pray—that is the only answer, for our God can bless and heal our nation, again. Oh, God in heaven, reach down from heaven and hear our crying hearts, that you will take back our land and bless it in the name of your Son Lord Jesus.

34

LIKE THAT OLD saying "God willing and the creek don't rise," our God is that bridge over the troubled waters that is threatening our bankrupt and trouble country and its people. This country of ours is seeing lots of troubled waters, and we don't want the floodgates to be opened up higher by the federal government and make the situation any worse. By the time our Forty-Fourth President leaves office in January 2017, our national debt will be almost $20 trillion. That is growing at a rate of $500 million per day. It seems that our president always wanting more money for his budget. That means more waste in spending and higher taxes. Where and when will all this wasteful spending ever stop?

God wants His church and our nation, the USA, be one that has victory in Jesus. We need more churches and for our country to be built on a solid rock with very strong foundation and good cornerstones. Pray that America will change from its sinful and wicked ways, that God from heaven will have mercy and hear our crying heart by blessing and healing our country again. Otherwise, we will be seeing our great America blowing in the wind.

"Return to Me, and I will return to you," says the Lord Almighty (Mal. 3:7).

Our America needs an old-fashioned revival reaching from coast to coast, for all churches to come together as one body in Jesus's name for the main purpose that God will hear our crying hearts and daily prayers for getting our America back to become a faithful country again. We don't need or want any "lukewarm" churches in our land. We must preach the whole Word of God from the book of Genesis to the book of Revelation till Jesus comes for His Church. Let's rekindle those revival fires in Jesus's name.

It takes faithful and hardworking people to make a true nation. We have come a long way as a faithful nation. We don't want changes from the dreams, hopes, principles, and the faithful visions of our Founding Fathers of 1776. Those believing principles are: "One nation under God" and "In God we trust." We still and want to believe in the principles of the freedom of religion, the freedom of the press, and the freedom of speech. Let's ring the Liberty Bell each day for all Americans of our land who still want freedom and liberty in our beloved America. Our Lord Jesus wants His church to be alive and His church in victory. Our Jesus wants this America to be alive and this nation to be in victory. Is our God sending a message or a warning to our country, the USA, to change our sinful ways? Now is the time to be in prayer each day for our America.

The good news is your Heavenly Father knows what you need before you ask him. If you look around, you will find corruption, greed, moral decay, and a steady decline of what made our nation so great. The principles of our Founding Fathers of 1776, "In God we trust," is the real backbone and heartbeat of our nation. I am asking you to join me in praying for our America. Remember that God is in control and holds the future of our country in His hands. Don't be afraid of asking for big requests for nothing is too big for our God in heaven.

Like in the old days when the twelve disciples were asking Jesus to teach them how to pray, my brothers and sisters in Christ, let's start with the Lord's Prayer. These are two of them:

> Our Father in heaven, hallowed be your name, your kingdom come, your will be done on earth as it is in heaven. Give us today our daily bread. Forgive us our debts, as we also have forgiven our debtors. And lead us not into temptation, but deliver us from the evil one." (Luke 11:2–4)
>
> For if you forgive men when they sin against you, your heavenly Father will also forgive you. But if you do not forgive men their sins, your Father will not forgive your sins. (Matt. 6:14)

Now is the opportune time for Americans to join together in prayer for our nation. The burden of America is heavy in these trying times, but our God is sovereign. He is more than able to bring repentance and revival fires to this land that we so love.

My church Colonial View Baptist, Cookeville, Tennessee, Preacher Al Gaspard, now retired, mailed out 122 letters before the national election of 2012 to all local churches asking them to come together to pray for our nation. Our church put up "In God we trust" in big letters on all four sides of our Putnam County Courthouse. Every courthouse in our nation should have those same big words "In God we trust" inside and outside of their building. It's up to each church across the nation with pastors, preachers, and priests to preach the good news of what the people need to hear, not what they want to hear for it's in your hands. At the same time, the church pastors should have the congregations across this country praying for our political leaders, that those leaders will have the hearts and minds that they might know God's way of equity and justice with wisdom.

> If any of you lack wisdom, he should ask God, who gives generously to all with out finding fault, and it shall be given to him. But when he asks, he must believe and not doubt. (James 1:5–6)

With the 2016 national election coming up in the next several months, we must pray that our good God will give our new leaders—the Forty-Fifth President and the members of Congress—greater wisdom. This took place during the time for Solomon when he asked for wisdom from God, and it can happen today as we pray for greater wisdom for our government leaders.

> O Lord my God, give your servant a discerning heart to govern your people and to distinguish between right and wrong. For who is able to govern this great people of yours? For God was please and said "I will give you a wise and discerning heart. (1 King 3:9, 3:12)

Let's get on our praying knees and look up toward heaven as we take the following words of God to our Father in heaven:

> The Spirit of the Lord will rest on him- the Spirit of wisdom and of understanding, the spirit of counsel and of power, the Spirit of knowledge and the fear of the Lord. (Isa. 11:2–3)

For our nation become humble, let's heed the words by Rev. Billy Graham: "To get our nation back on their feet, we must get down our knees."

> "So I say to you: Ask and it will be given to you; seek and you will find; knock and the door will be

opened to you. For everyone who asks receives; he who seeks finds; and to him who knocks, the door will be opened." (Luke 11:9)

"Because you have so little faith. I will tell you the truth, if you have faith as small as a mustard seed, you can say to this mountain, Move from here to there and it will move. Nothing will be impossible for you."

"I tell you the truth, if you have faith and do not doubt, not only can you do what was done to the fig tree, but also you can say to this mountain, 'Go, throw yourself into the whatever you ask for in prayer." (Matt. 17: 20-21)

Praise the Lord, O my soul, and forget not all his benefits-who forgives all my sins and heal all my diseases. (Ps. 103:2–3)

Be patient, then brothers and sisters until the Lord's coming. You too, be patient stand firm, because the Lord is coming near. (James 5:7–8)

See how the farmer waits for the spring to plow and sow the seeds of his crops and the autumn rain for his harvest. He has patience in his labor, because there will be products of his labor. The same with us believers, that we have the same kind of patience as the farmer, let's stand firm and tall in our beliefs.

> "Yes, I am coming soon." Amen, Come, Lord Jesus.
> The grace of the Lord Jesus be with God's people. Amen. (Rev. 22:2122)

> "All authority in heaven and on earth been given to me. Therefore go and make disciples of all nations, baptizing them in the name of the Father and of the Son and of the Holy Spirit, and teaching them to obey everything I have commanded you. And surely I am with you always, to the very end of the age. I am coming soon," (Matt. 28:18–20)

Two thousand years later, from the time of Christ first coming as a child and Savior to the world, how much sooner now will we be believing and hearing "I am coming soon." Thank you, Lord Jesus. We are ready, waiting, and watching for your coming to take your church.

In the meantime, the church of our Christ should make every effort to preach the Gospel of God's grace before the Rapture, so that many will be taken at the Rapture, thus escaping the horror of the Tribulation. Our nation is in need of a widespread revival in order to awaken the people of this nation. That all the churches come together in the name of Jesus to pray for our America. Lord Jesus, hear our hearts crying that you reach down from heaven and touch our praying hands. Our Lord wants His church to be in victory, and he will bless our nation in victory, if only we change from our evil ways. Lord, bless our country and place it on solid ground. Only God can bless and heal our nation again.

Lord, have mercy on us and our country.

We are living in the end-times and last days of His church age.

Come, Lord Jesus, for we don't want your church and America to be blowing in the wind.

> But those who hope in the Lord will renew their strength. They will soar on wings like eagles, they will run and not grow weary, they will walk and not faint. (Isa. 40:31)

Jesus wants His church to be alive and one in victory.

Jesus wants His nation to be alive and one in victory.

My dear friends, our America is in trouble. In my lifetime, I have learned that no political party or person is the answer. The only hope for our country is our Almighty God and our Lord Jesus. It's time to pray, that our God will hear from heaven to bless and heal our country.

> "If my people, who are called by my name, will humble themselves and pray and seek my face and turn from their wicked ways, then will I hear from heaven and will forgive their sin and heal their land." (2 Chron. 7:14)
>
> "Yes, I am coming soon." (Rev. 22:21)

35

MY FIRST WIFE died of colon cancer in October 1993. She was only fifty-two years old. We had a good marriage of thirty-two years being together, in love with each other, having two sons and a daughter. The next year, I divided the US Atlas of the USA into four sections to travel that year. I drove along and traveled in all forty-eight states, taking four different trips. In 1995, I got this Sheltie puppy. I named her Sunshine, and we became the best of friends, doing things and traveling together. She was named after that 1939 song by Jimmy Davis "You're My Sunshine." During all that time, I was single and lived alone with my Sunshine for six years. Most of the time, we went to church, visited my special friends of the Pacesetters, and spent time with my family and friends, and traveled.

One day as I was walking in my neighborhood with Sunshine, I started to pray to God for a lady to come into my life.

Oh God, I come to you in Jesus's name that you send me a lady to come into my life. Lord Jesus, this is what I want from you: a Christian lady that is attractive, caring, and kind, medium build, retired, and likes to travel. I will accept her family as she accepts my family.

I always went to the Cookeville Library a couple times each week to read the *Wall Street Journal* and various business articles. This time I picked up the Nashville newspaper, the *Tennessean*, and as I was going through the paper to the business section, there in front of me were two full pages titled "It Takes Two"—one full page of men looking for women and one full page of women looking for men. As I was looking at those single people's ads, I said to myself, *Say I can do that.* And I mailed an ad to that paper.

About three days later, when I got back home from the grocery store, there was a message on my phone. The phone message said, "Saw your ad in the paper. I believe that we have something in common. Please call me." That night I called that number. Nancy and I talked about our background and our family for over ninety minutes. She lived a hundred miles away in Bellevue, Tennessee, and was a retired nurse. As we talked, she said that they had lived in Greencastle, Indiana, for few years. I told her that Putnam County of Greencastle was where I was born. Next she told me, she was a nurse at the local prison, and I told her my brother-in-law works there. Yes, as you might know, she knew him. Her husband died of cancer eighteen years before we met, and she was more than ready to start a new relationship with a man.

We met here in my hometown of Cookeville as she came here two or three times each month to visit with her mother-in-law who lived here in an assisted seniors' living place. We had lunch together, and we talked for about ninety minutes, more and more about us and our family. We dated for one year and wrote daily love letters and visited each other often. I always wondered what my mailman and her mailwoman were thinking as they delivered those love letters each day.

The good news is that our families were all for our relationship. We got married on July 4, 1999, at her United Methodist Church in Bellevue. We were so much alike, easygoing and never had any disagreements. We took a few yearly small trips visiting with our family and friends in Indiana, North Carolina, and Virginia. Took one big trip each year going various places such as Alaska, Northeast and Northwest Canada, Europe, Ireland, and Scotland. We both got involved doing our family tree, making trips to different cemeteries and libraries. That was the main reason we were making the trip to Scotland, for that is where both our families came from.

Yes, our God in heaven heard our prayers, for I know for sure that He heard and answered all my prayer requests. Nancy's dreams, hopes, and prayers must have come true as well. Our Good God turned out to be a very good matchmaker, for we had an outstanding good marriage of twelve years. She died March 2011, at age seventy-six. It was super great while it lasted.

Thank you, Lord, for all the blessings in my two marriages.

My personal advice to older or young couples is to date each other about year in order to know each other better. This is a must, date and married a Christian person. Otherwise, it's hard to change those old ways of an unsaved person, only by God and many prayers. God will answer your prayers regarding dating and marriage, just asked and you will receive. I been there and done that twice because I know for sure about "It takes two." As a couple read together in your Bible the Song of Songs by Solomon. It's a love story of Love and Marriage between King Solomon the riches and wisest man ever and that of a country woman. Husbands always be so kind to that new bride and your wife in all the years to come, treat her with the Love of Christ. Your wife will become like the Lilly in the Valley or like that of the Rose of Sharon to her husband, for this God will bless your marriage. You both must make your marriage become holy and sacred as you build together the foundation of your love for each other. Only God can provide the kind of love for you both that your marriage will become like His blessing and promise, that of "His banner over us was love." Just remember, there will be times for giving and not of taking, always say I am sorry, and I was wrong. Take time to talk it over of any difference, next Kiss and make up. What great love mystery that God has given to single man and a single woman with marriage that they both become one.

> Therefore a man shall leave his father and mother and be united to his wife, and thy shall become one flesh. (Gen. 2:24)

There is a love song that came out few years ago, I purchase the tape at Christian bookstore for my wife; so we can share it together in our "Golden Years." Name is "Come grow old with me."

The next two years after my second wife died, I moved back to Cookeville to live with my daughter. Then, it was time for me to move on with my life. My daughter and I drove around Cookeville so that I could find a nice and safe place to live. We visit three senior citizen community living places for people of my age group. God picked Heritage Pointe Community for me to live, now I am happy that God done this for me. While living here, God lay on my heart to write this book, "America, Blowing in the Wind." He was the one give me the ideas and words to write for you to enjoy and learn about what has happened to our country and that of the near future of His coming for His church. Yes, it happened again, "It took two, God and me."

36

IT'S THE HOME with both parents—a husband and a wife—that forms a good family relationship. The parents should always be the backbone and the heartbeat of providing good Christian relationship with their children. This is made real by going to church each week and doing things together as a family. Being a good parent is a privilege, a responsibility, and a challenge—parents need to be helping their children to walk in the ways of God. A faithful and strong Christian family that goes to church creates a stronger America. Let's reach out to the children by bringing back those kind words "How are the children and grandchildren?" As the children go, so goes our America by creating a greater culture. It gives me great joy and pleasure to find some of our children and young people are walking in both the faith and the truth of God, just as our Father in Heaven command us to do. Just live for your faith each day.

Father Edward Flanagan said, "Often it has been said that youth is the nation's greatest asset. But it is more than that-it is the world's greatest asset. More than that, it is perhaps the world's only hope."

The greatest thing parents can and should do for their children is to plant or sow faith seeds in their hearts and minds. College and sports are not the most important things in the world for your children. As parents, let your children know, more than anything else in this world, that you want them to become faithful Christians.

All your sons will be taught by the Lord, and great will be your children's peace (Isa. 54:13).

Marriage involves Christian commitment between a man and a woman to each other for as long as they both live. This is from your wedding vows, "until death do us apart." Always make sure you are growing with the Holly Spirit in your Lord Jesus, for He will help your marriage that it become more alive and stronger. With true love for each other, you will have a good or great marriage. One of the biggest problems married couples or parents have is that of how to manage their money. Just sit down together around the kitchen table and make out a good yearly budget by each month that you both can live with. When that time comes of having children, there will be a big change in your budget planning, so plan wisely. Just remember there is no perfect marriage. Always talk it over to address any difference of what to do with your problems and how to solve them. It's always better take those family and financial problems to the Lord in prayer. In time, He will provide you with a good answer. Also, it's best talk with your pastor and get his/her viewpoint as you face those dark storms in your marriage. Husband and wife, or as parents, read your Bible and pray together each day with your children. Here is good starting point: Ephesians 5:22–33, 6:1–4. Also, read the book of John with your family.

There will be lots of those little sweet talks in your marriage years, just remember tell your husband, your wife, your children, grandchildren, and rest of your family/friends those three words—"I love you" or "we love you." Those words must come from your own heart. What a big difference that will make in those people lives, for they will know for sure that someone cares for them. Just as God loves us, we must love others with kindness. How strong is LOVE, it reminded me of the love story of Jacob who work a total of fourteen years for his future father-in-law, Laban, in order to have his younger daughter Rachel become Jacob wife. Those fourteen years seemed like only a few days to Jacob because of his love for Rachel. You can find that love story in your Bible in Genesis 29: 15-30.

There is another love story in the Bible that of Boaz and Ruth, found in the book of Ruth. It's a story of Naomi and her daughter-in-law Ruth returning to Bethlehem. When the landowner, Boaz, went out to survey his fields, he shouted to the workers, "The Lord be with you!" The workers shouted back, "The Lord bless you!" There in those grain fields, Boaz and Ruth meet, fell in love, and married. Yes, in this love story and in your love story, the Lord will be with you and the lord will bless you and your marriage. Just look in your Bible of the word, Love, there must be hundreds of Bible verses related to that one word. God had a deep purpose of and for the reason of Love.

God is the power of wisdom. Just ask in Jesus's name He will give you and your family the following: faith, hope, love, salvation, and wisdom. Just build your home and your marriage on a solid rock. Don't be afraid. Always be strong and in good courage, for He loved you first even before you were born.

You want to build your house and life on a solid rock for your family, not on sandy soil. Just like the Bible story of the wise and foolish builder. That way, your house and your life for your family will be built on a rock with good cornerstones and a solid foundation.

> Be like the wise man who built his house on the rock. The rain came down, the streams rose, and the winds blew and beat against the house, yet it did not fall, because it had its foundation on the rock. The foolish man built his house on sand. The rain came down, the streams rose, and the wind blew and beat against the house, and it fell with a great crash. (Matt. 7:34–37)

> The Lord himself goes before you and will be with
> you, he will never leave you nor forsake you. Do not
> be afraid; do not be discouraged. (Deut. 31:6)

My dear brothers and sisters in Christ, always be caring, kind, and humble with each other, and do it in love. Just be like our Lord Jesus as He washes His disciples dirty feet, for He did it in love.

> It was just before the Passover Feast, Jesus would
> showed them the full extent of his love. He got
> up from his meal, took off his outer clothing, and
> wrapped a towel around his waist. After that, he
> pour water into a basin and began to wash his
> disciples feet, drying them with the towel that was
> wrapped around him. (John 13:4–5)

God laid on my heart to write this book, *America, Blowing in the Wind*. He is the One who gave me the words to write down for you to read and study regarding the end-times, or last days, of His church age. Saving the best for last, I want take the time to pray for you, your family, and your friends. In order for you be caught up in the Rapture of His church, you must be *born again* or *saved*. Jesus came the first time to save us from our sins and give us salvation. The next time, Jesus will be coming in on a big white cloud for the Rapture of His church. As good parents, be sure that your children are born again or saved in Jesus's name.

You are not aging; you are ripening to perfection. Mark Twain said, "Age is an issue of mind over matter. If you don't mind, it doesn't matter." Our thoughts can greatly affect our mental and physical health, which can affect our aging process. Some older people are more positive and optimistic in their lifestyle that they act and look much younger than their age. While someone else that is younger, but who is negative and pessimistic seems to be both more inactive and have more health problems. Just take care of your body and mind. Be more healthy by eating the right food, drinking more water, and staying active. Keep in mind that old saying "An apple a day keeps the doctor away." Read your Bible daily with your wife and family, for it is the food for your soul and for the spirit.

We can't stand still. When our lives bring us joy or pain, we have so many days, months, and years in our lifetime. When you get to a certain age or are in your golden years, life is like an hourglass. There is more sand at the bottom than at the top of the hourglass. Time is marching on for all of us. The life span for a person on the average is about seventy years. I don't know why some people die at a young age. My first wife was fifty-two years old and my oldest son was forty-seven years old, respectively, when they died. Here I am, eighty-plus years old and going strong and still in good health for my age.

Sometime during our lifetime, it would seem as though we are in a dark storm, or at a crossroads, with nowhere else to turn. We get to a point where we cry out, "O Lord, here I am for my family needs you." We don't know what the future holds in our lives. Have God take you out of the valley of those dark storms and take you all the way to the mountaintop in victory. From the mountaintop, shout with joy, and He will give you living peace, and you will be saying, "Thank you, Jesus, for your healing hand has taken away all those heavy burdens off my back and out of my life. God knew us before we were born. He made us years ago, and He is still making you and me. Our Lord Jesus is the Prince of Peace.

Jesus can calm those dark storms in your life, just like he did for the twelve disciples on the Sea of Galilee. Our Lord Jesus is the master of all storms, for he will get in your boat with you and your family. As He is calming the waves in your dark storms, He will turn that small boat into a lifeboat for your safety and give you living peace. Like the Bible story of Jesus calming the storm for the twelve disciples, He can do it for you.

> A furious squall came up, and the waves broke over the boat, so it was that it was nearly swamped. Jesus was in the stern, sleeping on a cushion. The disciples woke him and said to him, "Teachers don't you care if we drowned?"
>
> He got up, rebuked the wind and said to the waves, "Quite! Be still!"
>
> Then the wind died down and it was completely calm. (Mark 4:37–39)

God is always there for you and your family. If your life seems to be in the fiery furnace, it might be like the story in the Bible when King Nebuchadnezzar demanded that people must bow down to his gods or be thrown into the blazing furnace. There were three Jewish men named Shadrach, Meshach, and Abednego who refused obey the king to worship his gods. Yes, our God is always there for you and your family, even in the fiery furnace.

> If we are thrown into the blazing furnace, the God we serve is able to save us from it, and he will rescue us from your hand, O king. These three men were firmly tied, fell into the blazing furnace. Then King Nebuchadnezzar leaped to his feet in amazement and asked his advise, "Where there three men that we tied up and threw into the fire?" They replied, Certainly, O king." He said, "Look! I see four men walking around the fire, unbound and unharmed, and the fourth look like a son of the gods."
> (Dan 3:17, 3:23–26)

We must pray for revival fire—that our families have greater faith, that we have greater family relationship, and that we keep our families together in both good and bad times. Let's rekindle those revival fires for our families. It's praying time in America for good family values. The latest polls show that 40 percent of American families are without fathers. How sad that this has come to this. Someone once asked Ruth Graham, the wife of Billy Graham, how she raised five children. And she replied, "On my knees."

How true that is. Only by praying. It's not easy having a family in this up-and-down world. May the good Lord be with you always.

Peace I leave with you; my peace I give you. I do not give you as the world gives (John 14:27).

Our life can be like driving a car in the fast lane, without any brakes. Most people in this modern age of the twenty-first century don't know when to stop and take the time to "smell the roses." Our Lord Jesus can take those trouble thorns out of your life and turn your life beautiful as a rosebush without any thorns. Just take your family problems to the Lord in prayer, for He will walk with you and talk with you in the garden of seeing the dew on the roses.

There are 137 women in the Bible, only 2 who have books in the Bible. They are Esther and Ruth of the Old Testament. Housewives and mothers are just like those two ladies. Because of her great faith, Queen Esther of Persia saved the Jewish people from death. While Ruth was a humble and gentle young widow, she cared for her mother-in-law and worked hard in the fields. Both of these women changed history in their day. Ruth had a baby who became grandfather of King David and the ancestor of our Lord Jesus. My dear housewives and mothers across our nation, pray in Jesus's name for faith, hope, and love, just like Queen Esther and Ruth.

You may be facing so many unknowns in life as to what to do next. These are some of those:

- Loved ones sick with cancer, diabetes, and heart disease.
- Loved ones having problems with alcohol, drugs, gambling, and pornography.
- Marriage problems leading up to divorce.
- Child and women abuse.
- Single parent raising children.
- Losing a child or grandchild due to death.
- Taking care of an elderly parent.
- Problems with forgiveness and how to forget.
- Layoff from work due to company financial cutbacks.
- Loved ones who are not born again or saved

Turn these problems over to the Lord Jesus. He will provide you with the right answers and touch your life with His healing hand.

A Good book for you to read is *When Your World Falls Apart* by Dr. David Jeremiah. He wrote about his experience with cancer of 1994. It was his bend-in-the-road experience, of how God healed his body and headed him back onto the road toward a greater ministry. Also in this book are other stories of people facing live problems and how God turned their lives around. Dr. David Jeremiah can be seen on Christian TV each Sunday and during the week of his Christian program *Turning Point*.

May the good Lord Jesus reach down with His healing hand to touch your body and make you whole again. In Jesus's name be healed. He will bring healing and good health back into your life. If you are worried about so many life problems, such as your family, finances, health, or the future, God is there for you anytime. If your life is burdened, just look up to heaven as you are kneeling down, and ask your Lord Jesus, "These burdens are too heavy for me to carry." Our Lord Jesus will do more than that, for He will carry you and all your burdens on His back. He is always there for you and your family. Just pray and He will come into your life today. All you need is to have faith as small as a mustard seed. Just believe, and you will receive that healing miracle.

Whatever your needs are, our God is there for you anytime. All you need to do is pray in Jesus's name. Just ask, and you will receive. God always loves you and your family. Your needs for yourself and your family may be like the story in the Bible of the widow's oil. God took care of the widow's financial debt and saved her sons from slavery. It doesn't matter if your request is big or small, your Father in Heaven is there for you and your family. Don't worry about anything. Just pray about everything. Our God is greater than all your needs.

The wife of a man from the company of the prophets cried out to Elishap, "Your servant my husband is dead, and you know that he revered the Lord. But now his creditor is coming to take my two boys as his slaves."

Elisha replied to her, "How can I help you? Tell me, what do you have in your house?"

"Your servant has nothing at all," she said, "except little oil." Elisha said, "Go around and ask all your neighbors for empty jars. Don't ask for just a few. Then go inside and shut the door behind you and your sons. Pour oil into all the jars, and as each is filled, put it one side." They bought the jars to her and she kept pouring. When all the jars were full, she said to her son, "Bring me another one." Then he replied, "There is not a jar left." Then the oil stopped flowing. She went and told the man of God, and he said, "Go, sell the oil and pay your debts. You and your sons can live on what is left." (2 Kings 4:1–7)

Do not be anxious about anything, but in everything, by prayer and petition, and with thanksgiving, present your requests to God. (Phil. 4:6)

My prayer for you and your family is that you will obey God's commands in your lives. May your home, health, and loved ones prosper under God's care and love. The following verses taken from the Bible may be helpful as you and your family are facing those crazy, unknown days or dark storms in your life. After our great God has answered your prayers, just start each day praising the Good Lord, and He will put much joy in your heart, mind, and soul.

> You will again obey the Lord and follow all his commands I am giving you today. Then the Lord God will make you most prosperous in all your work with your hands. (Deut. 30:8–9)
>
> For the Lord comforts his people and will have compassion on his afflicted ones. (Isa. 49:13)
>
> When you pass through the waters, I will be with you; and when you pass through the rivers, they will not sweep over you. When you walk through the fire, you will not be burned; the flames will not set you ablaze. (Isa. 43:2)
>
> "If anyone is thirsty, let him come to me and drink. Whoever believes in me, as the Scripture has said, streams of living water will flow from within him." (John 7:37–38)
>
> "A new command I give you: Love one another. As I loved you, so you must love one another." (John 13:34)
>
> The Lord is my strength and my shield, my heart trust in him, and I am helped. (Ps. 28:7)
>
> A righteous person may have many troubles, but the Lord delivers him from them all. (Ps. 34:19)
>
> Give all your worries and cares to God, for he cares about you. (1 Pet. 5:7)

> Be kind and compassionate to one another, forgiving each other, just as in Christ God forgave you. (Eph. 4:32)

The following are some of God's words to uplift those loved ones in your life that want to be born again or be saved before His coming in the Rapture:

> For God so loved the world that he gave his only Son, that whoever believes in him shall not perish but have eternal life. (John 3:16)
>
> "I am the way and the truth and the life. No one comes to the Father except through me." (John 14:6)
>
> "Most assuredly, I say to you, unless one is born again, he cannot see the kingdom of God." (John 3:3)
>
> Whoever believes in the Son has eternal life, but whoever rejects the Son will not see life, for God's wrath remains on him. (John 3:36)
>
> "I have come that they may have life, and that they have it to the full." (John 10:10)
>
> "You may ask me for anything in my name, and I will do it." (John 14:14)
>
> The kingdom of God is near. Repent and believe the good news. (Mark 1:15)

To repent is to change your heart, mind, and your life, to rid it of the sins of your past life. You will be preparing yourself for the ways of the Lord in your heart—that is to say, "Lord Jesus, I will live for you."

> But we ought always to thank God for you, because from the beginning, God chose you to be saved through the sanctifying work of the Spirit and through belief in the truth. (2 Thess. 2:13)
>
> Search me, O God, and know my heart; test me and know my anxious thoughts. See if there is any offensive way in me, and lead me in the way everlasting. (Ps. 139:23–24

Therefore, if anyone is in Christ, he is a new creation; the old is gone, the new has come. All this is from God.

> "In the time of my favor I heard you, and in the day of salvation I helped you. I tell you, now is the time of God's favor, now is the day of salvation. (2 Cor. 6:2)
>
> In Him we have redemption, through His blood, the forgiveness of sins, according to the riches of His grace. (Eph. 1:7)
>
> Those who wait on the Lord shall renew their strength; they shall mount up with wings like eagles. (Isa. 40:31)
>
> Not wishing that any should perish, but that all should reach repentance. (2 Pet 3:9)

Being born again or saved, Jesus will give you the blessed hope with new joy in your heart and peace of mind, for Christ is the Prince of Peace. Because Christ lives in you, there will be showers of blessing from heaven for you. Since Jesus is the light of the world, we should carry that light into our hearts and lives. The Lord is your rock, your fortress, and now your deliverer. He is standing on the rock for your salvation, and his banner over you is love. You are precious, God will never leave you and will answer your prayers.

What must you do to be born again or be saved?

First, acknowledge and confess that you have sinned against God. Second, renounce your sins, and do not go back to your old ways. Third, by faith receive Christ into your heart. It's always best to surrender completely to Him early in your life, so you can have all that wonderful joy and living peace in your heart, life, and soul most of your life. At this moment, you can receive the Lord and Savior in your life and have all the hope and joy in your heart, mind, and life.

Just get on your knees and pray these words with your heart, mind, and soul all in Jesus's name.

> O God, I am a sinner and want to turn from my sins. I believe Jesus Christ is your Son for He died on the cross for my sins and you raised Him from the dead. I want Him as my Savior and to follow Him as my Lord from this day forward, forever and forever. Lord, come into my life and fill me with your Holy Spirit in Jesus name, Amen.

> God will hear that simple prayer, for the Spirit of God will come into your heart. Even if you are lying on a sickbed and you never made your peace with God, it is still not too late. The dying thief on the cross turned to Christ and said, "Lord, remember me." And Jesus replied, "Today you will be with me in Paradise" (Luke 23:42–43).

Just as soon you repent of your sins, you have received Christ as your Savior. Your name will be written in the Lamb's Book of Life. You will be on your way to heaven after the Rapture of His church.

Death has always been the greatest unknown, and at times for some people, it's the greatest fear. Our Jesus won over death by returning to life, for he gave us Christians the victory over death. Thank God that the Resurrection of Christ did happen and that we can live again with our Lord Jesus.

> Death has been swallowed up in victory.
> "Where, O death is your victory?"
> "Where, O death is your sting?"
> (1 Cor. 15:54–55)

I know death from experience. My dad was dying from lung cancer in 1973. Rev. Charles Corey and I drove from Marion, Indiana, to Indianapolis for my dad's salvation. I am most thankful that I made that trip, knowing for sure that my dad was saved. A few weeks later, I did my dad funeral services, and years later, I did the funeral services for my two wives and my oldest son. With prayer, the good Lord gave me the right words to say at those four funerals, for I wanted my family and friends to hear and know about our Lord and Savior.

When my first wife died, we were at the cemetery that day in October 1993. I'd written the Twenty-third Psalm on small sheet of paper to read over her grave, and as I finished reading it, a gust of wind took it out of my hand, and I never saw it again, for it must have gone up into heaven for my wife to have and keep. That was one big experience for me, of the missing Twenty-third Psalm on paper that was blowing in the wind.

> The Lord is my shepherd, I shall not be in want. He makes me lie down in green pastures, he leads me beside quite waters, he restores my soul. He guides me in paths of righteousness for his name's sake. Even I walk through the valley of the shadow of death, I will fear no evil, for you are with me; your rod and your staff they comfort me. (Ps 23:1–4)

This is a good time for you to sing a couple great songs: "Amazing Grace" and "Go, Tell It on the Mountain":

> Amazing grace how sweet the sound that saved a wretch like me I once was lost but now I'm found was blind but now I see.

> Go, tell it on the mountain, over the hills and everywhere;
> Go, tell it on the mountain, that Jesus Christ is born!
> While shepherds keep their watching, O'er silent flocks by night,
> Behold thru' out the heavens there shone a holy light.
> Down in a lowly manager, The humble Christ was born,
> And God sent us salvation that blessed Christmas morn.

Thank you, Jesus, for my/your salvation. What a blessing of all blessings, what a promise of all promises, these words are from our dear Lord Jesus for today, tomorrow, and forever. It's an awesome power of praising our Lord, for the healing, for taking away the heartaches, and for our salvation. Praise the Lord and rejoice always, for it brings much joy and greater peace of the mind and soul.

> Be joyful always. Pray continually; give thanks in all circumstances, for this is God's will for you in Christ Jesus. (1 Thess. 5:16–18)

I wish to leave all Americans with these final words:

Grow in the grace and knowledge of our Lord and Savior Jesus Christ. Let's make every day of your life as if it is Easter, for the risen Christ wants to come into your life today. It's Friday, but Sunday's coming. Go to church every Sunday with your family.

To him be glory both now and forever! Amen (2 Pet. 3:18).

Keep looking up. God will meet us in the air.

Leave a trail of kindness. Is anybody happier because you have passed in their path of life? Will God will say, "You have earned one more tomorrow by the work you did today"?

Sing to the Lord a new song for He has done outstanding things for you and your family. The good news is that you and your family are born again, saved by the Grace of our dear Lord Jesus Christ. After your salivation, the most important thing is that you and your family are on your way to heaven. The good Lord Jesus will be there in heaven with open arms, saying to you all "Will done my faithful sons and daughters, welcome to your Heavenly Home."

Disclaimer

REFERENCE TO MY book, *America, Blowing in the Wind* is my own opinion, and the Bible verses are taken from the NIV Study Bible.

CPSIA information can be obtained
at www.ICGtesting.com
Printed in the USA
FFOW05n1458050916